Andy Butler

The Rustlers of Panther Gap

Scot Butler

The Rustlers of Panther Gap

GILBERT MORRIS

Tyndale House Publishers, Inc.
Wheaton, Illinois

Originally published April 1985 as *Barney Buck and the Flying Solar Cycle.*
Scripture quotations are from the *Holy Bible,* King James Version.

Library of Congress Cataloging-in-Publication Data

Morris, Gilbert.
[Barney Buck and the flying solar cycle]
The rustlers of Panther Gap / Gilbert Morris.
p. cm. — (The Ozark adventures ; 2)
Previously published as: Barney Buck and the flying solar cycle.
Summary: Thirteen-year-old Barney Buck places his faith in God and in a solar-powered flying bicycle to help his new Indian friends catch a gang of tree rustlers.
ISBN 0-8423-4393-8
[1. Mystery and detective stories. 2. Indians of North America—Fiction. 3. Inventions—Fiction. 4. Christian life—Fiction.]
I. Title. II. Series: Morris, Gilbert. Ozark adventures ; 2.
PZ7.M8279Ru 1994
[Fic]—dc20 94-7128

Printed in the United States of America

99 98 97 96 95 94
7 6 5 4 3 2

TO STACY

"Favour is deceitful and beauty is vain,
but a woman that feareth the Lord,
she shall be praised."

Contents

1
New Challenges

JAKE! Jake! Will you stop that infernal racket?"

I'd gotten up early to work on that algebra I was flunking. Then, just as the *x*'s and *y*'s were starting to make a little sense, I was blasted out of my chair by the sudden explosion of noise that my maniac of a brother called music!

I got up and yanked the door open to yell at Jake, regretting for the millionth time that I had agreed to let him buy those awful drums! As always with his nutty schemes, he'd set me up and sucked me into this one so smoothly that now the idea was somehow all mine and he was just an innocent bystander.

I waded through the room that had once been a

screened-in porch. All I could see were a pair of drumsticks whirling around over a stack of snare drums. I reached out and snatched one of the flashing sticks.

"How do you expect me to study with all this noise?" I demanded, trying to keep my cool.

"Well, for cryin' out loud, Barney! How can you expect me to win the contest if I don't practice? I mean, after all, it was *your* idea!"

Jake was built more or less like a fireplug. Even when he jumped, he didn't come up very high to me—I was built like a telephone pole. Jake had black hair and sharp, black eyes that threw off sparks whenever he got mad, which was pretty often. He looked like our great-grandmother, who was mostly Cherokee—a fact I never liked to talk about.

I was extra tall for my age, which was thirteen. With my red hair and awful freckles, I could never be mistaken for a Cherokee. Our youngest brother, nine-year-old Joe, was fair and blond like Mom and didn't show that Cherokee strain either.

"Barney!" Jake protested. Every year in Little Rock there was a band contest with a thousand-dollar prize. Jake had decided his group could win.

As he stood there, I wondered how he could think so much like a big-time con man. I'd spent a whole lot of time trying to get myself out of messes that Jake had gotten me into, and now he was trying to make me believe the drum business was all my fault!

"... and you were the one who said it would be great if I could get a group together and win that thousand-dollar contest in Little Rock this year."

"Don't blame it on me!" I replied. "You were the one who decided you were a musical genius! You decided to buy all this stuff. Why I agreed to spend good money on a bunch of drums, I'll never know!

Jake opened his mouth to argue some more, but worried that he might win this one as he usually did, I cut him off.

"All I said was the only way all this band stuff would be worth a dime was if you could win that contest—which you can't!"

"Sure I can, Barney." He nodded stubbornly. "We got a swell group! And I just thought of the perfect name for it!"

"Oh? What's the name?"

"Jake Buck and The Mistakes!" He swelled with pride, waiting for me to admire the name.

"I think that's *exactly* the name for your group!"

"I knew you'd like it, Barney. I have this flair for names. You gonna give us the money for the instruments?"

"We're not going to spend our money on a bunch of 'mistakes,'" I said.

He glared at me and muttered under his breath, "Well, there are other ways." After a pause he said, "I've been thinking about the five hundred dollars the Darrows have put up to anyone who'll ride that bucking horse of theirs. I figure five bills would about get us what we need."

I stared at him. "If you get on that horse—'Cyclone' they call him?—what few brains you may have will get knocked out! He's already busted up half a dozen pretty fair riders."

But I wasn't really worried about Jake getting on a wild bucking horse. The one thing he was afraid of was large animals.

Mrs. Simpkins, our housekeeper, came in from the kitchen carrying plates of eggs and biscuits. She interrupted Jake's argument by saying, "You boys better eat. The bus will be by in ten minutes. Where's Joe?"

"I thought he was still in bed," I said. "I'll bet he's out in his laboratory working on his invention."

"Yeah, he is," Jake said, sitting down. He reached for a biscuit, but Mrs. Simpkins rapped his knuckles with the handle of a knife.

"Ow! That hurt!" he cried, sucking his fist.

"You wait and say grace like you've been taught," she said sharply. Just then, Joe came through the front door, letting in a gust of cold air. Mrs. Simpkins grabbed him and plunked him down into his chair. "You better not let *me* catch you going out to that dirty old shed, young man! Most likely you'll get the flu, and we know who'll have to nurse you through it! Now all of you, please sit down!"

We waited until she put the rest of the meal on, then I said a quick blessing. Mrs. Simpkins had said it was up to me to set the example since I was the oldest.

We had Sheriff Tanner to thank for getting Mrs. Simpkins as our housekeeper. It's kind of complicated to explain, but our parents had been killed in a car wreck in Chicago the year before. We were about to be put in different foster homes when Jake thought up this big scheme about coming to Goober Holler to live in the old home where our dad had grown up. The house in Goober Holler was about seven miles from Cedarville—away from civilization, practically.

Well, we went through with it, but the judge in charge of kids like us said we had to have an adult living with us until we could get adopted or something. That's when Sheriff Tanner hired Mrs. Simpkins. Her husband had been dead for five years, and she'd been living alone. She was getting too old to live alone, but she was good enough for the judge in Chicago.

When we brought Mrs. Simpkins home, Sheriff Tanner said, "Barney, she's a gift from the Lord, the way I see it. Respectable as a church, Mrs. Simpkins is. And a good cook, too!"

That was all I wanted to hear. None of us were really into cooking—I could do it, but I certainly wasn't interested in doing it every day—and we'd do anything to keep from getting taken back to Chicago and put in foster homes, so it had worked out fine. Really, though, you'd have to say we took care of her, rather than the other way around! She did the cooking, but most of the time she was propped up in front of the TV, watching soaps. Still, she was nice, and I was glad we had her.

Now we gulped down breakfast and ran for the bus that stopped on the highway about a quarter of a mile from our house. It was late, and while we were waiting, Jake started up again.

"Barney, you *gotta* let us buy those instruments! How are we gonna win that contest with the old stuff we got now?"

"No! And that's final!" I said.

Jake's face got red. "Why is it you always let Joe get stuff for that old laboratory of his and you never let me have a dime?" he shouted. "You don't even know what he's making in there. Probably some kind of bomb that'll blow us all up!"

"No, that's not right, Jake," Joe said.

Joe had a ready smile and never lost his temper with anyone. He had a severe reading problem, what the doctors called dyslexia. Even though he was smarter than Jake and me put together, he had a real hard time reading. His teachers were good to him at school, and we all kept hoping he would be all right.

What Joe did was invent stuff—anything he could think of. He'd make switches that opened and closed windows automatically and all kinds of things. He'd worked in the house until he had an accident with a rocket. It went through Mrs. Simpkins' bedroom while she was reading the book of Revelation in the Bible. She'd thought it was the end of time and was spitting mad when she found out she was going to have to wait to go to heaven after all.

I gave Joe a punch and smiled. "Joe makes his own money—and it's not another rocket, is it, kid?"

"No, but it's a secret, Barney!" he answered.

Just then the bus pulled up.

Usually the bus was only half-full, but this morning it looked crowded. As we got on, Jake asked, "Who are all these strange kids, Barney? I don't know half of them."

"It's the kids from the school over by Panther Gap, Jake. Don't you remember the driver told us about having to make a longer run? That's why he's late, I guess."

"Yeah, sure, I remember," Jake grumbled as we got on. "Said they were going to close that little school and consolidate it with ours. Country-looking bunch, aren't they? That one looks like he lost his job on 'Hee Haw'!"

"Be quiet! They'll hear you!" I hissed, noticing that some of them already had.

Jake and Joe plunked down on the only seat left in the front. I saw one near the rear, next to one of the new kids, a small, dark-haired girl. I lurched toward it and sat down without looking at her—the way you do with a new kid. I did notice that she was pretty!

Pretty girls used to get me all gummed up. When we first got to Goober Holler and I met Debra Simmons, I really made a sap out of myself! But she'd been as much fun as some of the guys, and now we got along fine—for the most part.

I did have to explain to her once that she wasn't my girlfriend. Debra was real smart, but didn't seem to understand that I thought of her as just a buddy. She just gave me one of her heavy-lidded looks that made me feel all warm and uncomfortable. "Hmmmmm, if you say so, Barney."

Anyway, I thought that since I could act halfway human around one good-looking girl, another one wouldn't give me any problems.

I was wrong.

"Hello. My name is Robin. Robin Leatherwood."

I felt a light touch on my arm and turned to face her. Then I knew I was in trouble!

She had an oval-shaped face, with eyes big and brown as a doe. Her hair was black and came down in a little point on her forehead in what Sheriff Tanner called a "widow's peak." It fell down her back in two thick braids. Her skin was smooth and clear, a sort of ivory shade, and she had full, red lips. She smiled, showing the whitest teeth I'd ever seen and a little dimple on her right cheek. She had a soft voice and breath as sweet as honey. She was prettier than a speckled pup.

Looking at her that close was like getting an elbow in my stomach! I tried to say, "Hi! My name is Barney Buck," but what actually came out was "Gor-meeboo boggle!"

She must've thought I was the village idiot just riding with the school kids for fun. Even so, she just nodded and rocked me again with one of her dimpled smiles.

Very carefully, framing each syllable with the utmost precision, I finally got out, "Hi, I'm Bar-nee Buck!"

Great! Now she thought I had a speech impediment!

She batted lashes that were long enough to dust off a piano. "It's our first day at the new school. I've never been to any school except the little one at Panther Gap. I . . . I think I'm a little scared!"

I knew the feeling. When we'd come down from Chicago, I'd been scared to death.

"Hey, don't worry, Robin," I said. "It's a good school. The kids are real friendly. Why, my brothers and I started coming here just a year ago, and it seems like we've been here all our lives!"

"But what if they play tricks on me?" She bit her lip.

I made my voice deeper and gave a shrug like some

tough guys I'd seen on TV. "Look, anybody gives you any trouble, you come to me."

Her eyes opened wide and she drew a sharp breath. "Oh, my! You must be very important at this school!"

I tried to look modest and failed.

We talked almost all the way to school. By the time we arrived, she knew all about my dog, Tim, and how he was the best black-and-tan coonhound in the world, and about Jake's wild schemes, and that Joe was a genius with tools. I think she cast a spell over me. I never talked so much in my whole life! Especially to a gorgeous girl!

I was intoxicated, you might say. But just as we got off the bus, I came down to earth with a dull thud.

Robin pulled at the sleeve of one of the other new kids and said, "Barney, this is my brother Hawk."

Hawk turned around, and I knew right away the guy was an Indian. It was like meeting the last of the Mohicans face-to-face. He wasn't as tall as me, but he was muscled up the way I'd always wanted to be. He had black eyes, black hair, dark skin, and a hook nose. As far as I was concerned, the look in his eyes said, "Paleface, I scalp you!"

I realized then that Robin also was Indian. I had some Indian blood myself, but a lot of bad feeling to go along with it. My prejudice against Native Americans was based on what I knew of my great-uncle Frank.

Frank Tenkiller was Dad's uncle. Whenever he came to visit, he always ate us out of house and home. Worse than that, he drank! He once even stole money from my piggy bank to buy wine. Dad had always tried to excuse him, but I couldn't forgive him that easily.

All my disgust for Great-Uncle Frank must've registered on my face when I saw Hawk Leatherwood for the first time. He didn't say a word, but his jet-black eyes sort of glittered as he looked me over. Then he nodded and went on without a word.

Robin looked at him in surprise, then caught hold of my arm as we got off. "That's funny. Hawk didn't even say hi!" Then she looked up at me. "Barney, will you go with me to wherever I'm supposed to be right now?"

To cap the whole thing off, there stood Debra Simmons, watching me get off the bus with Robin hanging onto my arm. Debra had a good smile, but she wasn't wearing it as she took a long look at us.

Maybe if I'd just stopped and introduced Robin to her, a lot of the problems that swamped me later on would never have happened. But just as I was opening my mouth to say something, Robin pulled at me and said, "Oh, Barney, it's so nice of you to take care of me on my first day. I just know we're going to be real good friends!"

If I could've bottled the look Debra gave me then, I could've used it to poison rattlesnakes! I figured I'd find her and explain it all between classes, but she wasn't around anywhere. Usually we had a few quick conversations before lunch, then ate at the same table, but I didn't see Debra again until I went to the cafeteria.

I started to sit at our usual place. Then I glanced around and saw her at a table just behind ours, so I walked over.

"Hi, Debra," I said. "Say, I'll bet you're wondering—"

Just as I was about to put my plate down, somebody gave me a little shove. Rafe Darrow slid into the chair beside her.

The Darrows lived way back near Caddo Gap. They were mostly loggers, but the word was that they dabbled a little in moonshine and other stuff on the wrong side of the law. I'd never liked Rafe. He was good at sports and was real good-looking, but he was the kind of guy the town mothers warned their daughters about. He was two years older than me and looked almost grown up, while I still looked like a baby stork.

He grinned up at me and said in a deep voice, "You're in the wrong wigwam, Barney. Your tribe's over there. Good-lookin' squaw you got lined up—I'll say that!"

He motioned toward a table where the Leatherwoods sat alone. They were close enough to hear everything Rafe had said. Robin lowered her head. Hawk gave Rafe a black look and started to get up. I guess he'd have gone for Rafe right then, but Robin pulled him back.

Rafe laughed, and Debra said loudly, "How many

horses will her father want for her, Barney? Isn't that how the redskins do it?"

Now, of all the girls I've ever known, Debra Simmons was the kindest. She usually was the first to take up for an underdog. But she wasn't herself that noon, and the way her lips trembled and her cheeks turned red, I knew she wished she hadn't said what she did.

She wasn't the only one. I got so mad it made me dizzy! I did one smart thing. I walked away without a word and ate by myself. But I didn't taste a thing I ate.

How I got through the rest of the day, I'll never know. I went over the whole thing again and again in my mind until, by the last period, I saw myself as the innocent martyr and everybody else—Debra, Robin, Hawk, and Rafe—as the villains who'd ganged up to do me in.

It was no wonder I made such a jerk of myself in P.E. class. That was my last class, and when we went out on the court for a basketball game, the first person I saw was Hawk Leatherwood, wearing some ratty old gym clothes. Coach Dale Littlejohn was introducing him and Robert Skaggs to the guys.

I guess everybody has someone they want to be like. Coach Littlejohn was that for me. He'd been an all-American cornerback at Alabama and was as good-looking as Robert Redford. When my brothers and I had moved from Chicago to Goober Holler, Coach had become our closest friend. He'd gotten us to attend church, and even Jake (who usually had to be dragged to Sunday school) went without leaving any heel marks. Coach was a real teacher!

But there was one other thing: He was engaged to Jean Fletcher, the social worker in Chicago who'd made it possible for us to come and live in our home place. As soon as they married, they were going to adopt all three of us. What could be better than that?

Now Coach was telling us to make Hawk and Robert Skaggs feel at home in their new school. But did I listen? No, I filtered all that out. When we chose up, I managed to get on the team Hawk wasn't on.

You wouldn't *believe* what a sorry basketball player I was, even though I was the tallest guy on the court. Hawk, being new, was probably feeling nervous and out of place, but I shoved his face in the floor. It wasn't hard. I was so tall that all I had to do was give him a hip and send him reeling. When he went for a rebound, I'd nudge him hard enough to knock his feet out from under him. I got meaner and meaner.

When I looked around, I noticed all my friends were looking at me funny. I was usually the meekest guy on the court. "Barney, if you were a little more aggressive, you could be a much better player," Coach had always been telling me.

That day I was more than aggressive enough to suit

him! I sent Hawk crashing into the wall again. Coach blew his whistle and walked over to help Hawk to his feet. Then he gave me a look that ordinarily would've made me go through the floor, but I just stared right back at him.

"That was a foul, Barney," he said. "You've been getting away with murder today. You'd have been out of a real game long before this. What's the matter with you?"

I looked right at Hawk and said, "Why, I'm just being aggressive, like you're always telling me to be. But I won't have to be so rough now."

"Oh?" Coach asked quietly. Everybody was standing close so they wouldn't miss anything. "Why won't you have to be rough, Barney?"

"I found out that redskins are pretty soft," I answered, looking at Hawk and sneering. "No guts."

I tensed up, waiting for Hawk to jump at me. He could've mopped up the floor with me, but he didn't. He just stared at me, then dropped his head and walked slowly toward the locker room. A little mutter went around the group. I was happy I'd taught *him* a thing or two!

But I didn't really feel all that great about it. I'd been on the receiving end of a bully quite a few times, and what I had done was worse.

The guys broke up as the bell rang, but I didn't want to see Hawk in the locker room. I stayed behind, shooting free throws all by myself. Then Coach said, "Better shower, Barney. You'll miss your bus."

I figured he was going to bawl me out, so I said real fast, "Now, Coach, don't start on me! I know what you're going to say."

"Is that right?" He fixed me with steady eyes that were capable of paralyzing guys weighing over two hundred pounds.

"Yeah, you're going to tell me that I should've been nicer to that Leatherwood guy. But Coach, you've lived in small towns most of your life. I come from the big city, and I've seen how some people can mess you up if you let them."

Coach just stood there, and I got more and more rattled as I tried to explain how it was. "See, I *know* how Indians are. They're lazy and no good. You probably heard how they go crazy when they drink? Well, that's the way it is. I ought to know!"

Then I came out with my big evidence. "I hate to admit it, but I got some Indian in me. Of course, I don't go around *bragging* about it, and I think we got it pretty well under control. But, anyway, you got to keep them in their place!"

Coach was quiet. The longer he stood looking at me, the sillier I sounded to myself. I waited for him to pile into me, but he just stood there, disappointment written all over his face. Finally he left without a word.

Dad had done that to me a few times. I'd always wished he'd laid into me with a belt because that wouldn't have hurt as much as his silence.

I walked down to the showers, feeling as though a bad accident had caught up with me. There was only one guy left—Monte Walsh. Of all the guys I didn't like, he was probably number one. I considered him a dirty-talking sneak, but he ran up and threw his arm around me like I was a long-lost brother.

"Barney!" he said. "You really gave it to that redskin! Hey, kid, I like that! Keep 'em in their place, I say!"

That wasn't exactly my finest hour.

2

Narrow Escape

SMALL towns can be pretty awful for new people moving in. When we'd first come to Cedarville, we wanted people to stay away from us so they wouldn't find out we were just three kids living alone. But after things got straightened out, the townspeople accepted us just like we'd lived there all our lives. That was mostly because people like Coach Littlejohn and Sheriff Tanner and the Simmonses had led the way.

But lots of people just didn't like newcomers. Old Charley Peters, who drove the taxi, once said to a bunch of his cronies as they were playing checkers and spitting tobacco juice into a tomato can, "Why, nobody can say *I* ain't hospitable. I like *all* folks in this here town."

He spat in the can, then added quickly, "I mean all except them that has moved in!"

The new kids from the Panther Gap school had a hard time fitting in, but after a couple of weeks most of them had found their places and had made new friends. All except the Leatherwood kids. They were different.

Of course, our school was integrated, but there weren't any Indians at all in Clark County.

Hawk was in most of my classes, and I got reports on Robin from younger kids. The Leatherwoods seemed to be waiting for something. They didn't rush in to join us, and I decided they were just too stuck up. That's why I led the way in making things worse.

"They're just too good for us!" I said to Tony Randell one day after we'd watched Hawk leave the cafeteria with Robin. "They always sit alone, never doing anything with the bunch."

"I don't know about that," Tony answered slowly. He was a good-looking kid with curly brown hair and was one of the best basketball players in school. "Seems like we ought to make more of an effort to draw them into the stuff we're doing. They seem like pretty nice kids."

"They seem that way to you because you've never been around any Indians, Tony! Now I have, and let me tell you, they're a no-good bunch. Why, you just can't trust them an inch." I was thinking about my great-uncle Frank stealing the money from my bank.

Somehow I'd gotten the Leatherwoods mixed up in my mind with that.

"Best just steer clear of them, Tony. Indians don't care about mixing with us anyway. They're clannish, don't you see? Always with their own kind!"

Tony gave me a funny look, then shrugged.

I managed to swing the whole group around so that after two weeks neither Robin nor Hawk had any friends. I congratulated myself on saving my friends a lot of misery. They wouldn't have to get burned by those Indians firsthand now that I'd gotten involved.

One thing still bothered me—I couldn't get Coach Littlejohn to see my point of view. I tried to hint around, saying you had to be careful who you got close to, but he never seemed to listen. Instead he spent a lot of time with Hawk, and I overheard him say to one of the other teachers, "Hawk's goin' to be a winner. He's got more ability and smarts than any player I've had here."

Well, *that* didn't make me like the kid any better! Sure I was a pretty poor player, but after all, I *belonged!* I lost a lot of confidence in Coach about that time. I'd thought he had more sense, and here he was wasting his time on a kid who was going to wipe out sooner or later, just like the rest of them.

I went home that afternoon hopping mad at Coach, and I hurried to get my chores done. It was Friday, and I wanted to get away from the whole mess. Jake and Joe pitched in. As soon as we were finished, Jake started with the drums and Joe disappeared into his laboratory to finish whatever he was working on that was going to save the world.

Joe had his inventing, Jake had his drums, and I had Tim, my black-and-tan hound and the best dog there was. His head was almost black with a tan dot over each eye. He had a glossy coat and clear, keen eyes. He weighed about eighty pounds, and if there was anything more beautiful on this earth, *I* never saw it.

He did have a permanent limp, but that didn't keep him from being the best coonhound in the state, world, or anywhere else for that matter. Every spare minute Tim and I were out in the woods running coons, and I'd made a lot of money skinning them for the fur.

"C'mon, Tim. Let's get 'em!" I'd say, and like always he'd shoot out of the yard toward the woods, with me trailing him as fast as I could. Mrs. Simpkins knew I'd probably be out all Friday night, so she packed me a good snack and filled my stainless steel Thermos with steaming hot cocoa.

The coons had been a little thin around Goober Holler all fall, but Uncle Dave had said that over toward Caddo Gap they were thick as fleas on a dog. I made off in that direction.

It was almost dark by the time I got to Panther Gap. I decided to hunt that out, then go on to Caddo Gap the next day. Nobody would worry about me if I stayed out for two days and nights.

I felt like I'd been let out of jail. The woods were brown and crisp, and the deer were running like crazy, floating over logs in that graceful way they have. Tim and I just let ourselves go. It was looking like rain, but I didn't care.

I got reckless, maybe because school hadn't been too great. I didn't realize it wasn't a good idea to be reckless in country I didn't know. The area around Panther Gap was locked into the foothills of the Ozarks. By the time I climbed up one of those steep bluffs that shoot up out of the flatland—what they call the Gap—it was after dark.

It started to drizzle, and there was no moonlight at all. At first, I wasn't worried. Then the going got steeper, and Tim was off trailing a coon so that his bugle voice sounded far away like a ghost's. Then the sky really opened up! The rain came down in cold sheets, soaking me to the bone and making the rocks I was trying to scramble up slick and hard to hang on to.

I hadn't realized the mountain was so high, but I knew I had to be pretty well to the top. I'd been climbing a long time, and for the last fifteen minutes I'd been working my way sideways along a ledge. A blast of lightning nearly tore the sky apart. I looked down without meaning to and just about turned to jelly!

It must have been at least two hundred feet down—a

sheer drop— and the ledge I was standing on was less than a foot wide. Almost blind as a bat from the lightning, I clung to the side of the mountain like a leech. My heart was pounding like a drum.

I couldn't go back—it's always harder to climb down than up—so I went on. One inch at a time, I made myself go, feeling for the ledge, which seemed to be getting narrower all the time, and cutting my hands on the sharp stones of the ledge.

Finally the ledge just came to nothing, and there I was. The rain was awful! It filled my eyes every time I looked up. My fingers were so cold I couldn't feel them anymore. I knew I had to do something, but what?

While I was hanging there, I remembered something Coach had said in Sunday school just a couple of weeks before about Daniel in the lions' den. "There he was, right in the middle of trouble, and there was no method to help, fellas. He couldn't ring up a circus and get them to send a lion trainer. There wasn't a government program to help prophets in distress. There wasn't anything! So, Daniel did what he'd learned to do as a young guy—he called on the Lord. And the Lord shut the mouths of those lions!"

I wished I could change places with Daniel, but finally I just said a simple old prayer that sounded like a little kid's: "Lord, please get me off this mountain!" Not too eloquent, but it was sincere.

Just then another flash of lightning lit up the world, and I saw what I thought was an answer to that prayer—a ledge just about three feet away that looked like it led right to the top of the cliff about twenty feet over my head. I knew I'd have to jump for it. My fingers were so stiff I couldn't hold on another ten minutes. I waited for the next flash of lightning and threw myself across the gap toward the broad ledge. If it had been daylight, I couldn't have done it. I don't like high places. But there was no choice.

I almost made it, but not quite. My feet hit the ledge, and I made a wild grab for one of the scrub oaks sprouting out of the side of the mountain. Then the rock broke off beneath my feet. "No! No!" I cried out as I slid off the edge straight toward the rocks hundreds of feet below!

I thought it was all over. I knew I'd be dead in a few seconds. Then, instead of falling, I sprawled onto something hard. I grabbed a little oak that hit me right across the face, and I hung there in the darkness.

Lightning flashed again, and I managed to see that I'd landed on the *only* ledge between me and the rocks at the foot of the cliff. It was only a foot deep and not more than three feet wide, tapering off at the ends to nothing. I had a quick thought that God must've built this ledge as a "Barney-catcher," and I was plenty grateful for it.

But as soon as I was able to think straight, I got scared all over again. I was just about as bad off as I'd been before—maybe worse. By hanging onto the little tree, which wasn't any too strong, I could stay on the ledge, but I was just one move away from falling. I couldn't relax for a minute, and the rain seemed to be as cold and hard as ever. There was no way up and no way down. My only hope was that someone would come and get me.

Nobody knows where I am! I thought. *And they won't miss me until tomorrow, maybe even Sunday! I can't hang on for long!*

All my life I'll remember that night. How I hung on to that tree and thought a thousand times it was pulling out and I'd fall onto the rocks. How hungry I got because I'd dropped my lunch when I fell.

The Thermos helped save me. I had tied it around my neck with a leather thong. Every now and then I'd take a sip of that steaming hot cocoa, and it would wake me up. After a while I could hear Tim whining and barking, wondering why I didn't come on with him. I kept calling him, telling him to go home. If he showed up without me, they'd know something was wrong. But he wasn't about to do that! He stayed up there all the time, baying and whining in the rain and the dark.

Finally dawn came. I was ready to give up. My hands were like stone, and in the breaking red light of sunrise I could see that they were bleeding. The cocoa was gone. I was slowly slipping away from the ledge. I even had that feeling of warmth I'd always read freezing people get just before they die.

I didn't care much anymore. It would be over quick—just a little pain, then nothing. I was just about to let go when I heard a voice calling out to me.

Whoever it was seemed a long way off. I strained my head toward the top of the cliff and saw someone leaning out and shouting, but I couldn't make out the words. Then I saw Tim's head as he leaned over the edge. Finally in the early morning light I recognized Robin Leatherwood's braids. She stretched out her hand as if she could reach down twenty feet and pull me up with her tiny arm.

"Don't let go, Barney!" she said. "Hawk's gone for a rope! Just hold on for a few minutes. Please don't let go!"

She was all I had, and I didn't take my eyes off her. I would've fallen in a minute if I had.

After what seemed like a long time, someone else was beside me on the ledge. I looked into Hawk Leatherwood's dark face and felt him tying a rope around my chest. He told me to try to help as they pulled on the rope. Then he was gone. The rope tightened under my arms, and I was pulled to my feet. I wasn't much help. I could hardly grab the rope with my numb hands. Those two kids pulled me to the top of the cliff and saved my life all by themselves.

After I managed to get to my feet, I looked at Hawk

and Robin and changed my mind about Indians. I tried to say something, but my teeth were chattering too hard. They led me through the woods to their home. We were greeted by the best thing I'd ever felt in my life—a roaring red-oak fire. I traded my freezing clothes for some of Hawk's clothes, drank some hot soup, warmed up in the thickest featherbed you can imagine, and then dropped off into the deepest sleep I'd ever had.

I just had time to think, *Much obliged, Lord! Me and Daniel, we sure do thank you!*

I guess the Leatherwoods might've had trouble figuring that out, but God and I knew—and that was all that mattered.

3

Good Indians

WELL, looks like you're going to wake up after all."

For a minute I was scared because I couldn't remember where I was. Sitting up, I found myself looking right into the eyes of a woman I'd never seen, but I knew at once who she was.

"You're Robin's mother, aren't you?" I asked. She was just as pretty as Robin.

"Yes," she said with a smile. "You can get into your clothes if you feel like it, Barney. They're dry now. I expect you'd like something to eat."

She left the room, and I realized I was starving. Then I jumped into my clothes, which had been washed, dried, and ironed. I left the small bedroom and walked into a big room with a huge stone fireplace that was sending out warmth and making a cheerful crackling sound.

"Well, here you are, boy. I'm Glen Leatherwood," said a man sitting at the head of a table loaded with food. Robin was on his right and Hawk on his left. Mr. Leatherwood didn't look Indian. He was a trim, strong-looking man, about five feet ten and sort of wiry. He talked very fast.

"Guess you've met everyone else," he said, getting up and pulling out a chair beside Hawk and shoving me into it. "Now, Teena, let's get some grub inside this young feller!"

He rattled on like a phonograph, and I was glad because it gave me time to get my bearings. We were sitting in the living/dining room of their log cabin, and it was neat! Clay filled the chinks between the big logs. Two big windows on one side of the room looked onto one of the prettiest meadows I'd ever seen. The wall across from it was covered with snowshoes, traps, guns, and tools, most of which hung from pegs by leather thongs.

The fireplace took up one end of the room, and bookshelves sagging with books covered the other wall. All the furniture seemed to be handmade. The table was solid black walnut, polished and gleaming like glass. It was a room that looked lived in. *Loved in* was the funny phrase that came to my mind.

I glanced at Mrs. Leatherwood as she brought me a plate, then at the faces of Hawk next to me and Robin sitting across the table. Hawk's face was a little grim, but Robin had a smile for me. I tried to think what to say, and finally I asked, "How did you ever get me off that ledge?"

"Hawk rappelled down the rope and tied it onto you. Then he climbed back up and we pulled you up." Robin's face was gleaming with admiration as she looked at her brother. "Nobody else in the whole world could have done that!"

Have you ever felt you could walk under a door and still have room left to spare? That's how I felt then! Here I'd done all I could to put Hawk down, and he'd risked his life to save mine. I took a big swallow, turned, and looked right at him. He met my gaze, and I wanted to drop through the floor. Dad had always said if you have anything to say, say it. So, I did my best.

"If I'd been you, I'd have let me fall off that ledge," I said. "After the way I've treated you, there's no reason why you should have risked your life for me. Hawk Leatherwood, thanks for saving my life. If I can ever do anything for you, all you got to do is name it!"

My face was burning like a blast furnace by the time I got through. I could never keep a blush secret. In the first place my pale skin was covered with freckles that just jumped out when I got red. In the second place, there was a scar on my forehead just over my left eye-brow—a gift from Jake when he'd lost his temper and hit me with a shinny stick. Anyway, my whole face turned red as a lantern, and that dumb white scar showed up like a streak of lightning!

It got real quiet, and I finally glanced at Hawk. He was still staring at me hard. I thought maybe he was going to keep a grudge, but then his eyes lit up and he smiled. What a big difference that made!

"I'm glad we were around, Barney." That was all, but I knew that Hawk Leatherwood and I were going to be solid!

Mr. Leatherwood dropped a hand on his shoulder and gave me a smile.

"How'd you find me?" I asked.

"You eat, Barney," Robin said, passing me a plate full of smoked ham that made my mouth water. Hawk dumped some candied yams on one side of my plate, and Mrs. Leatherwood piled on a mountain of black-eyed peas.

Robin's dark eyes flashed as she went on. "We heard your dog, and at first we thought he was lost."

"That's right." Hawk nodded. "But I guess he really found *us,* Barney. We were on our way home from the river bottom and he came tearing up. He was making a lot of racket, and when we tried to take the old ox-road, he had a fit! It was just like something out of 'Lassie,'" he said with a grin. "Robin said, 'He wants us to follow him,' and I said that only happens in books, but she kept on. And that's how we found you. He led us right to the edge of that cliff."

I stared at Robin. "I'm glad you watched 'Lassie.' I'd probably be strawberry jam at the bottom of that cliff if you hadn't followed Tim. I guess you both saved my life."

She turned red then, but it wasn't a silly sort of blush like mine. It just made her a little prettier. She ducked her head, and her hands pulled at the little gold chain around her throat. "It wasn't anything," she said.

Well, we were OK from that time on. I stayed at their place all day Saturday, and they made me feel right at home. I was still pretty weak.

The Leatherwoods didn't have a phone, so I couldn't call home. But I explained how I mostly had to take care of myself, and that nobody would be upset if I didn't come home at any certain hour. That made Mrs. Leatherwood look sad. When I told her about losing our parents, there was a tear in her eye she didn't think I saw, but I did.

By late afternoon I felt good, but they asked me to stay and I did. Hawk had a coon dog named Tonto. He was a Red Walker and pretty good—not in Tim's class, of course. Still, the two dogs worked well together when we took them out for a short run. The place must have been swarming with coons.

Just that little time we spent together in the woods with our dogs made us friends. I'd never really had a best friend in Goober Holler—just lots of acquaintances. And if anyone had tried to tell me that my best friend would be an Indian, I'd have had him sent to the Oklahoma Home for the Silly! I think it was the same with Hawk, for I could tell that, under the mask he wore, he was lonesome, too. We were both talking like magpies by the time we got back to the cabin, making big plans for coon hunts and other stuff.

Robin met us at the door and smiled when she heard us arguing loudly about what kind of food is best for a coon dog's coat—arguing the way only good friends can. She said, "You sound like you're about ready to kill each other over these old dogs!"

Hawk gave her sleek black hair a tug. "Women don't understand these things, do they, Barney?"

"Heck, no!"

But I saw she was very glad that her brother and I were having a good time together.

After supper we all sat around the fire and played Clue. It was one of the best times I'd ever had in my life! We ate popcorn and washed it down with hot cider. Mr. Leatherwood told us a couple of stories from the war. He'd spent three years in combat in Vietnam, and some of the things he told made my hair almost stand on end.

"He got a bunch of medals he never lets anyone see," Robin whispered.

At about ten, it broke up. I sat in front of the fire with Mr. Leatherwood for a little while. That was when I found out why they lived so far from town.

Mr. Leatherwood was staring into the fire. "Barney, you sure are welcome. I've been worried about my kids—how they'd do in school."

"Why, they're both smart as can be, Mr. Leatherwood!"

"It ain't that, Barney." He shook his head slowly. "I mean, I've been worrying about how they'd get along with the others. Oh, they did all right at the little school here, but they don't seem to talk much about their new school at Cedarville."

My face burned, and I was glad he was staring into the fire. I knew it was mostly my fault they hadn't made any friends, so I said, "Gee, Mr. Leatherwood, it's just hard to get acquainted. Why, it took me and my brothers nearly a year to get used to a new school." That was true in a way, but it left out a whole lot!

"But it'll be different now, you'll see!" I continued. "Hawk and me, why we're gonna have the best time in the world, and I'll bet Robin gets in with all the girls right away." (I'd just decided that Debra could be a help with that.) "It's gonna be great! Why, I betcha they're gonna be the two most popular kids in Cedarville District."

Mr. Leatherwood looked at me with one eyebrow raised. When he saw how sure I was, he let go a deep breath. "Barney, I think you must be an angel from heaven! I really think you can help those kids, and they need it." I knew I didn't *really* qualify as an angel, but I was glad he thought so.

"Ever since I married Wahteena," he said, his voice almost down to a whisper, "I've had to worry about how my people would take it. And it's been hard. My own relatives have never accepted her as a member of the family. That's why I've stayed away from them and from most other folks."

"But, gee, she's the prettiest lady I ever saw!" I said.

"Me, too, Barney." He grinned. "Her name means 'spring flower,' and that's what she was the first time I saw her. But some folks only see that she's Indian."

"Well, it's not fair," I said indignantly. "People ought to have more sense!"

Pretty good coming from Barney Buck—the Bigot of Goober Holler!

"Well, it'll help Teena a lot, knowing the kids have you for a friend, Barney. I know she's been worried about them. And it's not just now—they've got a long way to go. You see, I intend for Hawk and Robin to have the best education money can buy."

He must have seen me looking around the modest cabin with the handcrafted furniture, because he laughed and waved his hand toward the walls. "Oh, I know you probably think I'm crazy, having such an idea. But it's all set, Barney. Their education is all paid for."

"You got it in the bank, Mr. Leatherwood?"

"Better than that. Banks go under sometimes, but my money won't go when they do."

"You have it buried somewhere?"

"No, not really." He gave me a smile. "It's in trees, Barney. Black walnut trees."

I looked out the window, but it was too dark to see anything. "Around here?"

"There are sixteen on this place, Barney, but I've got more. They're scattered all over Clark County."

"Sixteen? That doesn't sound like too many." I knew Mr. Simmons, Debra's dad, didn't think anything about cutting five hundred full-grown pines.

He smiled at me. "Know how much a mature black walnut tree is worth, Barney?"

"Well, I know a good pine can be worth as much as two hundred dollars—maybe even three if it's big enough."

He leaned back and watched my face. "Barney, a good, straight black walnut tree, fully grown, will bring as much as ten thousand dollars."

I guess my jaw about hit the floor. "Ten thousand dollars! Why, what makes them worth so much?"

"They're that valuable because they take so long to

grow, and there ain't many left. Takes ten years to grow a pine—twenty for a big tree. Takes fifty to seventy-five years for a black walnut to get its growth. And nobody's growing them. All the big timber companies want pine 'cause it's fast. They clear-cut the land now—just cut everything on it, and then plant the whole thing in pines." He frowned. "There won't be a hardwood tree in the state if those big companies don't stop."

"Who buys the trees?"

"Plywood companies. They can get enough out of one good tree to make a thousand bedroom suites. Cut it in real thin strips, then glue it on cheap wood. *Veneer,* they call it."

"Gee, where'd you get all those trees?

"My granddad had land all over Clark County, Barney. Most of it was in parcels of forty acres. He sold it off a piece at a time, but he did one thing—he kept a little plot and put out black walnut saplings. That was over sixty years ago. Now those trees are just ripe for the plucking. Most of them are on little one- or two-acre spots, but they're there—and that's what's going to get the best education in the country for Hawk and Robin."

Mrs. Leatherwood came back saying, "Barney, your bed is ready." Then she came close and put her hand on my shoulder. "I'm glad Hawk has a friend like you." Then her soft lips framed a smile. "And Robin, too."

Before I went to sleep that night, I made up my mind

that Hawk and Robin were my responsibility. I'd gotten them shut out at the school, and I would somehow get them in. I figured it wouldn't be too much of a job. So off to sleep I went—visions of sugar plums and happy Indian faces dancing in my head.

4

Temper, Temper

BUT Debra, all I'm asking you to do is be a little nicer to her!"

I had hunted down Debra the first thing Monday morning with plans of smoothing everything between her and Robin Leatherwood. Could anything have been simpler than that?

Of course, what probably made things a little tougher was my getting off the bus that morning arm-in-arm with Robin. As soon as I'd gotten on the bus, I'd squeezed into a seat with Hawk and Robin. Robin had ended up sort of sitting on half of each of our laps. We got just plain silly and, when we got to school, were still fooling around, pushing and shoving as we stepped off the bus. Robin grabbed my arm, and then we practically ran over Debra.

I opened my mouth to say hello, but Debra had done an about-face and vanished with a gaggle of her girlfriends. I turned to Robin and said, "I know you're going to like Debra. She's swell, and she's popular with the girls. If she likes you, you're in."

There was a funny look on Robin's face. "Maybe she won't like me."

I stared at her, then turned to Hawk. "Why wouldn't Debra like Robin?"

He cocked his head and gave me a steady look. "Barney, are you innocent or just plain dumb? You want your girlfriend to take another girlfriend of yours under her wing? Then I got to tell you about the tooth fairy and Santa Claus and all the other fables."

"Look, Hawk, Debra and I—well, I've explained that we're too young for all that stuff."

He gave me an unbelieving look. I made some excuse and said I'd meet him that night to go hunting.

I caught up with Debra just before third period. We usually met then to catch up on what was happening. She was talking to Betty Caldwell and another girl, but I knew they didn't have anything important to talk about, so I grabbed Debra by the arm and pulled her off to a corner. When I got her wedged in between the water fountain and a locker, I put it to her again as simply as I could.

"Debra, I really want you to be nice to Robin Leatherwood."

"Oh, is that right?" she asked, turning a little pink. Debra was tall, and sometimes I thought she liked me because she had to look way up at me. This time she straightened up like she wanted to tower over me. When she spoke, she didn't sound like herself at all.

"*You* want me to be nice to Minnie Ha Ha?"

"Debra, I wish you wouldn't call her that!"

She stared a hole in me with those deep-set eyes of hers. "Oh, you don't want me to call her that? Well, let me ask you, Barnabas Buck, who made that name up?"

Well, she had me. It seemed like a lifetime, but it really had been only a couple of weeks ago that I'd been such a turkey about the Leatherwoods.

"Well, I shouldn't have done it, Debra, and I'm trying to make up for it. Hawk and Robin are going to be my best friends."

Debra got redder still and began tapping her chin with one finger. Her eyes were sending off sparks.

"Oh?" she said in a mock-sweet voice. "So Minnie Ha Ha is going to be your best friend? Then you won't want to be bothered with *old* friends, will you, Barnabas?"

I knew I was in trouble when she called me Barnabas. What was wrong with her? Debra had practically saved my life when I'd first moved to Goober Holler.

I wanted Debra to say, "You're right, Barney. I *do*

need to be nicer to Robin!" Instead she said, "Barnabas Buck, you can take your whole tribe out of Goober Holler and stuff a possum up your nose for all I care! And don't you dare speak to me again as long as you live!"

Her face turned white as paper and tears glistened in her eyes. She whirled around and pushed by me. Some of the kids had heard her. It would take only a few minutes for the whole thing to get all over school.

Things went from bad to worse that day. Debra wouldn't even look at me, but it seemed like everybody was pointing at me and giggling. I half expected to see an item about my tiff with Debra in the school paper, in that dumb column about kids romancing: "What tall Yankee has split the blanket with a local beauty over a new gal with braids? Better put on the war paint, DS!"

It was partly to get even with the whole stupid bunch that I stuck as close to Hawk and Robin as I could. I told myself it was to set an example, but I was mostly feeling like a martyr. And the more time I spent with them, the more the kids kept away from all three of us. I guess they were saying about me what I'd said about Hawk and Robin: "Just too stuck-up to have anything to do with us common folks." It just about drove me crazy!

One ray of light at the end of the tunnel was Coach. He stopped me after basketball practice. His eyes were twinkling and he was trying not to grin. "I see you've had a change of heart, Barney."

"Aw, cut it out, Coach! I was all wet about that, but I'm trying to make up for it."

"Yes, I've noticed that, and I've told Jean about it. It's a good thing you got right. She was just about ready to come down from Chicago to work you over."

Since she was only as big as a kitten, that would have been funny to see, but I suddenly wished she were there. "When are you getting married, Coach?"

"Soon as she finishes that degree she's working on." He made a face, then grinned at me. "Why? You anxious to have a ma and pa to dump all your problems on?"

Actually, I did want something like that, but I knew it would be a year—maybe even two—before she finished. Then it would take forever for the courts to OK the adoption.

I just said, "Yeah, that's it. You wanna get some practice straightening out a nutty redhead?"

Coach suddenly put his arm around me and gave me a squeeze that nearly broke my ribs.

"I'm not worried about you, Barney!"

Except for my talk with Coach, the week went from bad to worse. Joe blew the windows out of the laboratory with some kind of gas. It nearly scared Mrs. Simpkins and me to death.

He came out with singed eyebrows and a surprised look on his face. "It's OK, Barney, I've got it now. Don't worry!"

"Don't worry!" I hollered. "You crazy kid! You nearly blew us up with your crazy invention! What in the world are you making in that place? An atom bomb?"

I never got anywhere fussing at Joe. He just gave me that gentle smile of his, and before I knew it, I was apologizing for getting a little upset about being blown to bits by his little old bomb!

Jake pestered me day and night about the new instruments. He was stubborn, and I knew if I didn't watch him like a hawk, he'd get me into something that would leave puckered scars all over my body.

"Barney, we even got a great new name for our group. . . ." He looked at me to be sure he had my attention, then said loudly, "And here they are, the greatest little group on this little old planet, folks, Jake Buck and The Swampdrainers! How's that grab you, Barney? Ain't it the *max?!*"

He grinned like an idiot, then rushed on, "And we got a great new song, Barney! It's a lead-pipe cinch to win that contest. It's about this girl who has a boyfriend who gets run over by a police car and dies."

I stared at him in disbelief. "What's the name of it?"

"'He Wears a Hubcap for a Halo!'" Jake shouted, pounding on my arm. "How can we lose with a song like that?"

"No, Jake! N-O! Do you understand me, Jake? Watch my lips, Jake. No!"

"In other words, you're not going to give me the money?"

"Not in *other words,* Jake! In *those* words. I will not give you the money for the instruments."

He shrugged and seemed to give up. But that should have tipped me off. He never gave up—not my brother Jake! He said something under his breath.

"What was that?" I asked quickly.

"I said 'there's always a way.'" He gave me one of his shrewd looks and added, "That five hundred that we can get for riding Cyclone . . ."

I grabbed his shirt front and gave him a shake. "You are not going to ride that crazy horse! You wanna get killed?"

He didn't lose his cool. Instead he just shrugged and said, "Well, I'm probably too young, and since you're the oldest, I thought you'd be the one." I glared at him and walked off in disgust. You can't teach a kid anything!

The good part of the week was that I spent every free minute with Hawk and Robin. We went out after coons every night. It was great sitting around a campfire in the middle of the deep woods listening to our dogs strike a hot trail. Better than any music I've ever heard.

One night Mr. and Mrs. Leatherwood went with us, and they were something! I thought I was pretty good in the woods, but even with my long legs, I had real problems keeping up with Teena and Glen. (I just called them that in my head of course, never out loud.) But that woman could glide through the woods like a ghost without a sound. And if Glen Leatherwood got around in 'Nam as quickly and quietly as he did on the trail, I'll bet he was bad news to the enemy!

We really got along. I even took Jake and Joe over there once, and they fit right in, too. The thought came to me that if Coach and Miss Jean didn't want us, why, it wouldn't be bad at all to have parents like Mr. and Mrs. Leatherwood.

But on Friday the roof fell in. It was like getting hit on the head twice, real hard.

In fifth period history class, Mrs. Henderson was telling us about how black people had struggled for their freedom. It was real cool! Mrs. Henderson had been on the march to Selma herself. She wasn't just beating her gums. I mean, she'd paid her dues! She tied everything together—the Civil War, the Revolution, World Wars I and II, Korea, 'Nam, and Selma—and it made sense, even to me.

"So, freedom has to be for *all,* or it doesn't exist," she said. She'd been talking for nearly an hour like a house on fire. Now, just before the bell, she spoke softly. "If there's one person—no matter what color he is or what church he goes to or how he parts his hair—if just one person is ruled out and put in a little box, and you write Not Free on that box, then there is no such thing as freedom."

It was real quiet. I looked over at Hawk and Robin. They both had solemn looks on their faces. Robin glanced at me and smiled.

I ducked my head and looked the other way—right into Debra's eyes. She was in the class, too, and right beside her was Rafe Darrow. They both had seen Robin look at me. My face grew red. I knew my white scar was showing like a flag, so I covered it with my hand like I always did.

"Say, Mrs. Henderson, can I ask a question?" Rafe said loudly.

He usually never asked anything except to go to the bathroom—so he could smoke.

Mrs. Henderson was a little surprised, but she nodded. "What is it, Rafe?"

He uncoiled a little in the desk and gave her a wide grin. *He's just showing off,* I thought.

"Well, you've been telling us all about how there ain't no real difference between folks—I mean, color and race don't really mean anything?"

"I didn't say *that,* Rafe, as you'd know if you listened once in a while. What I've been trying to say is that none is *better.*"

"Yeah, well, now there's one thing I've always heard—about Indians." The room grew still as a tomb, and my fingers were white where I was holding onto the desk. I knew he was trying to get at me through the Leatherwoods, but I hadn't dreamed he'd have the nerve to try it in front of Mrs. Henderson.

"Yeah, well, what I've always heard is that Indians can't hold their liquor—just go plain crazy. Now I know a *little* about stuff like that. . . ." He almost laughed out loud, and we all knew he was talking about the moonshining all the Darrows have always done. "And my question is—if there ain't no difference between people, why can't the redskins hold their liquor as good as a white man?"

I thought Mrs. Henderson was going to explode. She was a big woman, tall and heavy, and her face looked like a storm. She got control of herself, then said slowly, "Rafe Darrow, I hear those words, and all I can think of is Dachau and Buchenwald!"

I knew those were the names of concentration camps used by the Nazis in World War II—death camps where thousands of innocent people were killed in gas chambers. It sent the shivers over me, but I think Rafe was too ignorant to know what she was talking about.

Then the bell rang and I got to my feet. I was so mad I caught up with Rafe as he got to his locker, pulled him around, and stuck my face up into his.

Now, I was taller than he was, but that didn't mean a thing. He was thick shouldered and had a neck like a young bull. He could lift more weight than any kid in school, even in the upper grades. I knew he'd been on a

Golden Gloves team once and had gone to the semifinals. In a fight there wouldn't have been enough left of me to bury! But I didn't care.

"Rafe!" I shouted. "You are a low-down, dirty skunk! If a cat found you, she'd rake dirt all over your slimy body!"

Well, of course every kid in hearing distance rushed over to where we were and made a circle. People always push forward to see a bad accident, and I was about to become one!

Debra was standing there with her mouth open, trying to say something and not able to.

Rafe looked down at my skinny hand on his thick arm, then raised one of his black eyebrows and grinned. A sigh of dismay went around the group. They weren't going to see me get killed.

"I'll say this, Barney," he said with a smile. "You got nerve! You must know I could mash you into paste."

"Yeah, well, you just come outside, Rafe, and we'll see about that." I was proud of myself. My voice, which had been rather unpredictable, didn't break for once, and I was feeling nutty enough to add, "I better warn you I'm pretty good at judo and karate."

Translated, that meant I'd seen "Kung Fu" on TV a few times.

He just shook his head. "No, I don't think I'll take a chance with a dangerous guy like you. I've got my boyish charm to think of. The ladies wouldn't like it if I got scarred." He winked at Debra, then looked back at me. "Besides, Barney, since I heard what you're gonna do tomorrow, I guess you'll need all the strength you got. No need to waste any wrestling on me!"

I stared at him and dropped my arm. "What's that mean?"

"Oh, come on now, Barney, you might as well let everyone know what you're gonna do tomorrow." He raised his voice. "I guess you all want to get up early tomorrow even if it is Saturday. See, Barney is gonna ride Cyclone at the sale barn!" A hum went around, and both Debra and Robin whispered, "Barney! No!"

I wanted to do more than that! I wanted to shout from the top of the town hall: "I am not going to get on that killer horse!"

But just as I opened my mouth to deny the whole thing, I felt someone touch my arm. I turned and saw Jake. "Barney," he whispered. "I been meaning to tell you. . . ."

He didn't have to say any more. He'd arranged for me to get on that man-killer and win the money for his stupid instruments.

"Well, Barney," Rafe said lazily, "that will prove something, won't it? If you get on that horse, he may kill you, but you'll show you ain't a wimp. If you don't get on—well, what can you expect out of a guy who deserts his own kind?" He didn't look at Hawk or Robin, but everyone knew what he meant.

If I didn't get on that horse, I would be letting Hawk and Robin down—the two who had risked their lives to save me.

"Don't worry, Barney," Jake said. "I know you can do it!"

Maybe *he* knew that for sure, but the rest of the kids looked at me as if the lid of the coffin were ready to be nailed down!

5

Cyclone

I wouldn't speak to Jake on the bus ride home, or during chores, or at the supper table. He kept following me around, saying it was going to be easy!

Finally, just before we went to bed, I said, "Jake, you're too thickheaded to realize it, but you've signed my death warrant!"

He shook his head stubbornly. "I know you're worried about riding that horse, but it's going to be a breeze!"

"A breeze!" I stared at him, wondering how my own brother could be so dumb. "Jake, that horse has piled up four guys in the last two months—and two of them had done a lot of riding in rodeos. And now I'm supposed to get on that killer, and it's going to be a *breeze?*

Me, the guy who can hardly ride a bicycle, I'm supposed to ride a crazy bucking horse that even rodeo riders can't stay on?"

"Don't worry, Barney! It'll be all right," Jake assured me. But I'd heard that enough times to know better. Then he asked me, "Barney, have I ever gotten you in serious trouble with any of my schemes?"

That sort of stopped me. I tried hard to think of something.

"Well, I've never actually gotten killed, but I've come close! And this is the closest of all!"

I lay awake practically all night to keep from having nightmares about that horse. I thought about Uncle Dave, who'd done a little rodeo riding himself back in the old days.

"Son, there's horses that buck pretty bad 'cause they been trained to, and they ain't really no problem," he told me. "But some horses are born mean—just like some men—and they buck 'cause they want to get a man off their backs and stomp him. That Cyclone horse is like that. They ought to shoot him before he kills somebody—which he *will* someday."

Nobody but the Darrows would have gotten a kick out of watching guys try to stay on that horse. I asked Uncle Dave if they weren't risking a lot of money. They'd offered five hundred dollars to anybody who'd ride Cyclone till he quit.

"Ain't no risk at all, Barney," Uncle Dave said. "Now if they'd set a time limit, several could stick and get that five hundred. But that horse ain't going to quit. If he can't buck a man off, he'll rear up and fall over backwards on him. If that don't work, he'll scrape him off with a low tree limb or fence post. He'll get any feller that ain't got the good sense to stay off him."

I didn't want any breakfast the next morning, and Jake made a big joke. "The condemned man didn't eat a hearty meal!" And he wondered why I didn't think that was funny.

We caught a ride into town with Elder Franklin, the pastor of one of the rural churches. He was a tall, nervous man with a big Adam's apple that went up and down like a yo-yo when he talked. He kept looking at me, and when we got out, he said in a weak voice, "I'll be praying for you, Barney." He looked like he didn't have a wagonload of faith. As he let us out at the sale barn, he gave his long face a mournful shake.

The barn, the busiest place in the county on Saturday, was already packed with pickups and trailers. It had a big corral where they kept the young stock, but on the days when the Darrows brought Cyclone in to perform, they kept the corral clear. The manager of the sale barn was a Darrow himself and made money betting on how long the victims would stay on the horse.

"Barney! You come over here!" I looked up and saw

Sheriff Tanner talking to Mort Darrow, Rafe's father. The sheriff was mad as a hornet, and I knew why.

"Barney, you gone *crazy?"* he said angrily.

His face was red, and I hated to be the cause of it. He'd been real good to all of us boys, especially to me. He once had to arrest me for dognapping (which, of course, I hadn't done), but he and his wife took care of me in the county jail like I was in a fancy motel. One of the reasons that Chicago judge had let the three of us stay at Goober Holler was that Chief Tanner had gone to bat for us. He would've adopted us in a minute, too. Actually, he was chief of police now, but he'd been sheriff when we first met him, and I still had to get used to the new title.

"Chief, it's not my say," Mort Darrow said. Like his boys, he was a big, good-looking man and had a bad reputation in the county. "I just own the horse. I don't make nobody ride him. Now ain't that so?"

"No, you don't *make* nobody ride that animal, Mort," Chief Tanner said. "You just offer so much money that some of these boys bust their necks trying to get a hold of it."

"Boys will be boys, I reckon, Chief." Mort Darrow grinned. "You go right on and talk that boy out of it. It wasn't my idea."

Chief Tanner stared at him for a long time, then said, "You know, Mort, I'm going to get you someday."

Then he turned to me. "Barney, you're not riding that horse."

I was glad he said it. After all he *was* chief of police, and in a way, he was my guardian. I drew a deep sigh of relief. "Well, if that's what you want, Chief. . . ."

He nodded. "That's it exactly. Now, Mort, I'm warning you. Stop this nonsense before somebody gets killed!"

"Ain't breaking no law, Chief," Mort Darrow said easily, then turned and left us.

I felt good! I didn't have to get on that horse, and nobody could blame me. I was talking to the chief when all the Leatherwoods pulled up in their truck.

Mr. Leatherwood had a worried look on his face. "Chief Tanner, I gotta talk to you."

Chief looked surprised, but nodded. "Sure, you want to go to my office?"

"No, this will do," Mr. Leatherwood said. "Chief, we've got some rustlers operating around here."

"Rustlers?" Chief Tanner asked sharply. "You sure about that, Glen? I haven't heard of any stock that's been stolen."

"Not stock," Mr. Leatherwood said, "Trees."

Chief looked puzzled.

"Somebody's been stealing my trees, Chief. They got one sometime last week, a nice big one over near the county line at Kirby."

"Well, that's too bad, Glen," Chief said with a smile. "But one tree?"

"It was worth at least eight thousand dollars, Chief," Mr. Leatherwood said. Then he explained about the value of walnut trees.

Well, that shook Chief up. "Come on, Glen! We'd better go to the office. This is more serious than I thought. Tree rustlers! Guess I've heard everything now!"

Mrs. Leatherwood drove off with them in Chief's car. Hawk and Robin stayed with us at the sale barn. Hawk wanted to look at a cow.

We fooled around most of the morning. Jake disappeared somewhere, and Joe went to sit with Mr. Addison, the high school science teacher. Robin, Hawk, and I had a good time just looking at the stock. I didn't know one end of a cow from another, but they did, and I asked so many dumb questions it got us all sort of hysterical.

Chief came back with the Leatherwoods.

"Hawk, Robin," Mr. Leatherwood said, "your mother and I are going with Chief to where the tree was stolen. You can stay and go to that movie you were hoping to see."

If Chief hadn't been gone, maybe the whole thing wouldn't have happened. About an hour after he left with the Leatherwoods, the three of us ran into a bunch of kids from school. I was surprised to see Debra and Rafe among them. Rafe was at the sale barn most Saturdays, I guess, but I knew Debra hated the place because she'd told me so. And there were a lot of other kids who usually never went to the sale barn.

I took one look at Rafe and knew what was in his head. It was too late for me to run. He led the whole bunch up and said, "Well, you feeling good, bronc buster?"

"I . . . I'm not gonna be able to ride Cyclone."

He grinned. "I didn't really think you would, Buck." He stared at Hawk and Robin and added, "Like I said, a guy who don't know who his own kind is—why he ain't likely to have much in the way of guts."

That did it. I said, "If Chief Tanner hadn't told me not to ride that horse, I would—even if it killed me!"

Rafe grinned and draped one arm across Debra's shoulders. "You mean your daddy won't let you? Poor little feller!" Then he gave a loud laugh. "Look there, guys, one of them's red on the outside, and the other's yellow on the inside!"

I got so mad I went a little crazy. "Let's go find that horse!" I said.

A shout went up. Most of the kids began saying, "You show him, Barney," but I heard Robin whisper, "Barney, don't do it!"

I shook her off and led the way to the corral where

Cyclone was tied. Rafe must've told everybody I was going to ride, because just about everybody in the whole place was crowded around the fence. A mutter went up as I stepped inside.

Mort Darrow looked at me and said, "Why, son, you *know* what the chief told you 'bout that horse."

"He's just a fire-eater, ole Barney is, Pa," Rafe said. "You ain't gonna talk him outta riding Cyclone! Is he, Barney?"

I stared at Rafe. I would've given anything in the world to be somewhere else. I was hoping that Chief or Coach or *somebody* would come to keep me off that horse, but nobody came.

"Rafe Darrow, I'll show you that I'm not ashamed of my friends. And after I ride that horse, I'll whittle *you* down to size!"

All the men laughed, and most of the kids giggled.

I glanced at Debra. *Don't do it, Barney, please!* she said with her lips.

That nearly changed my mind, but it was too late. Rafe grabbed me and said, "I'll even help you get on, just to show I'm a good guy." He dragged me over to the post where Cyclone was tied.

Cyclone looked like he was asleep. But I'd seen him fool riders twice this way. He was like dynamite—pretty harmless until it blows up!

I had only one hope. That was to get on, get thrown

off, and scramble through the fence before Cyclone could get me. Both the guys I'd seen ride him had done that, although one of them had broken his ankle when Cyclone had stomped on it.

As I mounted, I wondered where Jake was. He'd been gone most of the morning. I glanced over to the rail, and there he was, with a big grin on his face, giving me a thumbs-up sign. I thought that he was a brother who ought to be put away! Here I was about to be killed, and he was grinning!

As I was getting settled on Cyclone, Jake suddenly scurried out and said something to a cattleman named Darren Pullen. Mr. Pullen was rich and had become a good friend of ours after we'd found his lost coon dog a few months before.

He listened to Jake, then said real loud, "Mort, where's the five hundred?"

Mort Darrow got red in the face. "You don't think I'm going to *need* it, do you, Darren?"

Mr. Pullen was a tall man with a face like a hawk. He said loud enough for everybody to hear, "I'm waiting to see if you're going to be an honest man or a welsher, a two-bit gambler who won't pay off, like I always said you were."

Men had gotten shot for less in Clark County. From the look old man Darrow gave Mr. Pullen, I thought he'd be smart not to ride around the Darrow place in the dark! But it worked.

Mr. Darrow pulled a thick billfold out of his overall pocket, took some bills out, and shoved them at Mr. Pullen. "Maybe that'll shut your mouth, Pullen," he snarled. Then he said to Rafe, "Turn that animal loose!"

Rafe untied the reins from the snubbing post and made a jump for the fence. I braced myself for the explosion. Just for a second or two, it was real quiet, like it is just before the free throw to settle a county basketball championship.

Everyone was waiting for Cyclone to blow up. I kicked my feet out of the stirrups and got ready to be launched like a rocket.

But *nothing happened!*

A gasp went up, because Cyclone didn't even hump his back. He took a couple of steps forward, then stopped and dropped his head almost to the ground.

"What's the matter with that horse?" Mort Darrow shouted, and a hubbub broke out among the crowd. I just sat there as he and Rafe came running over to where we were. Mr. Darrow picked up Cyclone's head and said, "What have you done to this horse, Pullen?"

"Looks like he went to sleep, Mort." Mr. Pullen grinned, and a little laugh went up from the crowd. That made Mort Darrow even madder, and he started to pull me off the horse.

"Wait a minute," Mr. Pullen said, "You're admitting you lost the bet, aren't you?"

Mr. Darrow stared at him. "There's something funny about this. Ain't nobody ever seen that horse act that way. I want my money back!"

"No, you won't get it!" Mr. Pullen said. "Not unless you want to take it away from me."

He was a pretty big man and looked like he *wanted* Mort Darrow to tackle him. I guess Mr. Darrow would have done it, too. If the Darrows were cowards, nobody ever found out about it. But Mr. Pullen was rich and had a lot of influence, so I guess that made Mr. Darrow think twice.

He yelled, "You ain't heard the last of this! I'll take you to court, you hear me?"

Mr. Pullen just laughed. "How long do you think it would take a Clark County jury to file against you for welshing, Mort?" Then he grinned at me and said, "Get down any time you want, Barney. You win."

A little cheer went up as I got off. Mort and some of the men gathered around Cyclone. Then suddenly I found myself sitting in the dirt, my head spinning like a top. I thought at first that Cyclone had come to and tossed me off.

When my head cleared, I saw Rafe standing over me, his face red. He said, "Get up, you little sneak! I'm going to teach you a lesson. Then I'll start on that buck and the squaw!"

I don't know how in the world it happened, but I got up and plowed into him, flailing like a windmill. He kept knocking me down, and I kept getting up. The world got pretty red, like I was looking through a curtain, and it seemed to me that some other people were getting involved. I found out later that Joe and Jake had grabbed Rafe's legs, Hawk had belted him from behind, and Robin had gone for his face with her fingernails!

Rafe must've thought he'd got caught in some dangerous machinery. But even then, he was so strong and tough that he put me down with a lick that sent the whole world turning.

Just then Mr. Darrow and a bunch of other men arrived to break us up. Too bad in one way, but good in another! I noticed Debra moving toward me, and I sure was glad. She was going to wipe the blood off my face, and things were going to be all right with us again!

That was what I'd hoped, but it didn't happen. Instead, Robin flew over to me, crying, and mopped my face with her handkerchief. When Debra saw that, she stopped like she'd run into a corner post. She bit her lip, and before I could even say a word, she turned and went over to Rafe Darrow, took out her handkerchief, and started rubbing his face!

She led Rafe off, and Robin led me off. Debra and I were right back where we'd started. Why did life have to be so blamed complicated?

6
Tree Rustlers

MY face healed up in a few days, but hurt feelings don't heal as fast as cut lips and black eyes. Debra avoided me at school, and that hurt my feelings. What a mess!

Even worse was the fact that she wouldn't stop being Rafe's shadow. I couldn't understand how a good girl like Debra Simmons could hang around a guy like Rafe Darrow.

Coach explained it to me once when I finally mentioned how much it bothered me.

"Barney, I know you're shocked that a 'good' girl like Debra is attracted to a 'bad' guy like Rafe. But Debra isn't all good, any more than Rafe is all bad."

"He comes pretty close!" I snapped.

Coach gave me a hard look.

"First it was Hawk. Now it's Rafe. Who's going to be next on your 'bad guy' list, Barney?" He shook his head. "One day I hope you'll start thinking about people as individuals, son!"

"But he's always into something—smoking, gambling, fighting . . . ," I said indignantly. "You know he is!"

"Sure, and I was pretty much like him when I was his age, Barney."

"You!"

"Yes, me! Until I became a Christian, I was pretty wild. Maybe that's why I can show a little more sympathy for Rafe. But lots of people are drawn to guys like Rafe. And most of them think they can reform them. Sometimes they can. I think that may be on Debra's mind."

"Converting the heathen?" I asked, then forced myself to grin. "Guess I'm just . . . just . . . oh, I dunno what I am."

"Just human, Barney," he said with a smile.

I hoped he was right, because the way Rafe was hanging on to Debra, I wondered if he wasn't closer to converting her than she was him!

At home things were a little better. Jake used the five hundred dollars to buy a bunch of new instruments. I couldn't tell that they made the band sound any better, but Jake claimed they did. He'd changed the name of the group again. This time it was "The Universe."

"Jake and The Universe?" I needled him. "You think that's big enough?"

"Ought to be about right, I guess," he said modestly. "Say now, we got this new song, Barney. It's about this guy who has a girlfriend who's a skin diver. She goes down and gets trapped by this octopus, see?"

"What's the name of it?"

"'I Lost Her to the Arms of Another.' Isn't that a kick?" He went back to his drumming and the moaning he called singing, and I knocked on the door of the barn that Joe called his laboratory. He came out, closing the door behind him.

"How's it going, Joe?"

"Almost finished, Barney. You're going to be surprised!" Joe was always happiest when he was inventing.

Mr. Addison had once said about Joe: "He's got a mind given to synthesis. That means he can take different things and put them together in unusual ways. He has a hard time reading, but he can see things in ways the rest of us can't. I think Edison was pretty much like that."

Well, you can't get much better than Edison! So I left Joe to his puttering around, while I spent most of the next two weeks in a tree.

That sounds as nutty as one of Jake's schemes, but I'd come up with an idea to help find out who was stealing the trees from the Leatherwoods.

Chief Tanner had told the Leatherwoods that the county sheriff was their best bet. "My authority is good only here in town, and I can't be out there looking for tree rustlers," he said.

I was at the Leatherwoods the day Chief brought the county sheriff and his deputy out to talk to them. "This is Thad Richards, the acting sheriff, and this is his brother R.D., his deputy." They both were big, nice-looking guys, wearing sharp uniforms. They looked like they'd been around. They sat down and began to explain the situation to the Leatherwoods.

"Mr. Leatherwood," Sheriff Richards said, "it's going to be real tough catching whoever's been taking those walnut trees. If they were all in one place, we could put a man out to watch until the rustlers came. But as you know, they're in fifteen little plots scattered all over Clark County. To be honest, I can't think of a way to do the job."

R.D. added, "It could be nearly anybody, Mr. Leatherwood. Look at how many guys in Clark County are loggers. Must be five hundred. You've got the equipment. Why, Thad and I do, too! There's a little sawmill down every path in this county, and plenty of guys who poach a few trees now and then!"

"But can't you do *anything?"* Mr. Leatherwood asked.

Sheriff Richards ducked his head and grimaced slightly. "We're going to do all we can, Mr. Leatherwood. I'm putting most of my hope in the forestry service. They have men out all the time, and I'm asking them to report any activity in the areas. And we're passing the word to the landowners in the nearby areas, telling them the same. Maybe we'll get a break. I sure hope so. It's a rotten thing to have happen!"

I was pretty hopeful somebody would get a lead on the tree rustlers, but the next week, three more trees were taken. The Leatherwoods didn't find out about it until they got word from a man who owned land close to their cabin.

"This isn't going to work," Mr. Leatherwood said. "We'd have to watch all the locations all the time!" He groaned. His wife looked ready to cry, and Robin and Hawk looked pretty glum.

Suddenly I had a great idea—maybe the first one I ever had. "Why can't we watch them ourselves?"

"Barney, they're scattered too far apart . . . ," Mr. Leatherwood said.

"Sure, but some are not far from where Felix Simpson lives," I added.

Felix was a big freshman who played football. Not all that smart, but a good guy.

"He could go over there once in a while and look at this bunch of trees.

"Why, some of the others are not two miles from where Ernie Jackson lives—he could keep an eye on those, couldn't he? And all of us could go by every day at different times and check the trees nearby. Why wouldn't it work?"

"You know," Mr. Leatherwood said, "it just might! That just might do it!" Then he picked me up and gave me a hard squeeze, which wasn't easy since I was the taller one.

Well, they thought I was a genius or something and put me in charge of the whole thing! I rounded up a bunch of guys—and some girls, too! We got more than half the stands of walnut trees assigned to kids, even though lots of them looked at me like I was crazy.

I ran myself into the ground, keeping as close a watch as I could on the trees I could get to. I was used to walking from all that coon hunting I'd done, but this was even harder. I wanted to do something to repay the Leatherwoods for all they'd done for me.

But it didn't work. After working as hard as we could during November, six trees were stolen. I was just sick over it, and so were the Leatherwoods. Mr. Leatherwood said that he'd probably cut the rest and get them to the mill before the tree rustlers got them. Over a fourth of them were already gone.

"Whoever's doing it knows trees," he said gloomily. "They've taken the best."

"Most people around here have been in logging in

one way or another," Mrs. Leatherwood said quietly. "It could be anyone."

"You need some expensive equipment to get big trees like that," said Sheriff Richards. "A log truck, a loader, at least. That means at least two men to do the job, maybe more." He shook his head. "I feel like I've let you folks down, but R.D. and me are spread pretty thin, you know."

"Not your fault, Sheriff," Mr. Leatherwood said. "Sure hate to have those trees cut, though. If I could let them stay in the woods for another five years until the kids get to college, they'd be worth more. Market would be a lot better."

"Hold off as long as you can," Sheriff Richards said. "I'm getting some money from the city council to hire some extra men if I have to bother them to death! Bunch of misers!"

The tree rustlers seemed to know exactly where to go. Even with extra help, seven more of the big trees were cut in the next two weeks.

It was late afternoon the following Friday when the Leatherwoods pulled into our yard. We all went out to meet them. I noticed that Mr. Leatherwood was feeling down.

"I just came by to tell you not to do any more watching, boys. I've decided to sell out."

"Can't we try for just another little while, Mr. Leatherwood?" I asked. "We'll catch them sooner or later."

"Can't wait, Barney," he said quietly. His shoulders were stooped like an old man's. "I'll have to take what I can get. It won't be what I'd hoped, but we have to take things like they come."

I wanted to say something to cheer him up, but I couldn't think of a thing. I looked over at Robin. She'd been crying. Hawk looked as if he'd *like* to. Mrs. Leatherwood didn't show any emotion, but I was pretty sure she was feeling just as bad as the rest of them.

All of a sudden I said something that surprised me as much as it did them. "Don't worry. God isn't going to let you down."

Now, if there was one thing I wasn't, it was a flaming evangelist. I had trouble "giving a testimony" in our little Sunday school class, and here I was, spouting like a prophet!

"What did you say, Barney?" Mr. Leatherwood asked, looking at me in a strange way. In fact, they all were. They knew I went to church, and I knew they didn't, but we'd never discussed it.

I cleared my throat and said again, "I know God isn't going to let you down. I've been in a worse place than this, and he didn't let me down. I know he thinks as much of you as he does of me."

Not much of a sermon, was it?

Mr. Leatherwood smiled and said, "Well, thanks for the kind word, Barney."

I could see he thought I was just being nice, but I wasn't. That was the funny thing! I had this strong feeling that no matter how bad things got, everything was going to come out all right.

They drove off, and I turned to look at my brothers, who were staring at me as if I'd grown an extra head. "What's the matter with you guys?"

Jake gave me one of his quick grins. "I hope you do better with your praying than I'm afraid you're not going to do."

I tried to unscramble that and couldn't do it.

I think Jake was telling me I was a fool for believing in something that couldn't happen. Still, I kept thinking about the ledge that had caught me as I was falling off the mountain that stormy night.

Maybe God had a little ledge for the Leatherwoods, too!

7

Too Close for Comfort

WELL, there it is. What do you guys think of it?"

Two days after the Leatherwoods had come by with the bad news, Joe took Jake and me out to his laboratory to unveil his brainstorm. Nobody had been permitted inside for over two months—except for Mr. Addison, who'd come to help a few times. I have to admit I was pretty curious!

Joe pulled open the big double doors and led us inside. "What in the world is it, Joe?" I gasped, looking at a strange contraption. He'd strung lights up all over the place, so I could see all right. I just couldn't make any sense out of it.

"It's the Flying Solarcycle, Barney! Ain't it *great?*"

I walked around the thing that looked like a cross between a monster kite, a gas balloon, and a glider. It had a long, cigar-shaped balloon running along a framework made of aluminum bars. But it also had a triangular-shaped wing above the bag and some sort of seat below—for the rider to sit in, I supposed.

"But what does it do, Joe?" I asked.

"Why, it flies, Barney! Can't you see?" Joe ran around it, explaining how it worked. "You sit in here, see? And you inflate the balloon with helium from this tank, see? And that makes it go up, and then the wings catch the air currents, and you glide on the updrafts!"

He was as excited as a young pup with his first coon. I just shook my head and stared.

"What makes the propeller turn, Joe?" Jake asked, pointing to an aluminum propeller mounted on a shaft that stuck out from behind the seat.

"Well, you can turn it with the pedals here." He gave a set of bicycle pedals a turn, and sure enough, the little propeller began to spin. "But that would be too hard. What really makes it go are the solar cells mounted on top of the wing."

"I don't see any cells," Jake said.

"Oh, no, they cost a lot," Joe said. "As soon as I save up enough, I'll buy them. Then the Solarcycle will be ready."

An idea was taking shape in my head. I walked around the fragile-looking thing.

"What did Mr. Addison say about this, Joe? Did he say it would fly?"

"Oh, sure," Joe said with a grin. "He said it could be marketed, and that it could take the place of an ultra-light. He wants to talk to some people about making a lot of them. But he said it has to be tested before we can get it patented."

"And you need the solar cells for that, right?" I asked slowly. I could see the perfect way to catch the tree rustlers! If the thing worked, I could just glide around all day, and aside from being fun, it would be possible to patrol the whole county. It couldn't miss!

"Look, we *have* to have those solar cells, you guys. Now, how can we get enough money for them?"

Joe told me what they'd cost, and I did some quick figuring.

"With what I can scrape together, we'll need at least another two hundred dollars. Jake, you got any of that five hundred left I risked my neck for?"

"Nooo," Jake said slowly, "but I know where we can get it. Joe, if I can get the money, I'm into this rig for half, OK?"

"Why, you—you chiseler!" I said outraged. "You'd do that to your own *brother?*"

"Do what?" Jake asked with a hurt expression on his face. "I'm just offering to help him, that's all."

I started to yell, but Joe said, "You can have a third, Jake. We all get a third of everything. We're brothers, aren't we?"

For once Jake had the grace to blush, and I enjoyed it. "OK, big shot, how do we get our hands on this money?"

"Well, you know old Mrs. Hooper? Widow lady who lives near Amity? She's got piles of money, but the coons have been eating her out of house and home. They got over half her corn this year, and she says if someone'll get rid of them, she'll pay them plenty!"

I let out a whoop that scared Tim half to death. "Coons! Hey, I was born for it! Why, Tim and I will clean those coons—"

"Wait a minute, you haven't heard it all," Jake interrupted. "Mrs. Hooper is a big animal lover. She's gonna leave all her money to some home for stray cats in Little Rock. Anyway, she'll only pay if the coons are caught without being hurt, and taken someplace where they won't bother people."

"What? That's almost impossible!" I cried out. "If you trapped them carefully, they could still get hurt."

"I know," Jake said, wearing that bragging look I hated. "That's why I'm so smart, Barney, and maybe after this you'll appreciate me!"

Oh, he was unbearable when he was like that! And he wouldn't tell me anything more. Every night for three nights he disappeared with Hawk, who drove his dad's pickup. Hawk drove Jake over to Mrs. Hooper's place and then back.

"I don't know what Jake's doing," Hawk mumbled. "He makes me wait in the truck, then goes off and does something. Won't tell me a thing!"

The next night, Jake said, "We do it tonight. Put the camper on the truck, Hawk. We'll haul the coons way over to Hot Springs County. Those gamblers there won't even notice a few coons."

All of us went, including Robin and Joe. When we got to Mrs. Hooper's place, it was still pretty light. Jake made Hawk and me carry some bags of feed, then led us out to a field.

We got to an open spot, and Jake said, "This is it. Mrs. Hooper raises the best corn in Clark County right here. Guess the coons found out about it. Besides, she doesn't allow hunting, so they're thicker than fleas on a dog."

He showed us some old saucepans that were pitted and dented. "We'll fill those with corn. I've been baiting them coons for three nights. They'll be along as soon as the moon comes up. Here, gimme some of that corn." He took a double handful, filled one of the pans, then took a small bottle out of his pocket. He opened it and carefully mixed its contents with the corn.

"What's that?" I asked.

"Jake Buck's Special Coon Catcher" was all he'd say. We followed him around and filled about two dozen pans with the feed. He treated them all with whatever was in the bottle.

Finally, he said, "Let's go back to the truck. We can build a fire and roast us some wieners."

"We don't have any," I argued.

"Sure we do! I brought them myself—and some marshmallows, too."

It was a good idea, I must say! We stayed around the truck for about four hours, eating marshmallows and hot dogs and having a party.

About midnight, Jake said, "Let's go get 'em. We might as well drive over there."

"Won't they run off?" Robin asked cautiously.

"When I catch coons," Jake said firmly, "they stay caught! Come on!"

We piled in the truck and drove to the field. I noticed some lumpy-looking shadows by the headlights of the truck. "What's that?" I asked.

"Coons!" Jake hollered. "Look at those coons!"

Coons littered the field, and they all looked dead.

"Jake, you poisoned them!" I said.

"Naw, I didn't. They're just asleep." Jake pulled the bottle from his pocket. "See that? I got a bunch of dog tranquilizers from Doc Fender, the vet. I crunched them all up and mixed them into the corn. When the coons got that corn, they got the tranquilizer, too. Look at those sleeping beauties!"

"Did you, by any chance, use that stuff on Cyclone?" I asked Jake as we got out of the truck.

He gave me a quick grin. "I refuse to testify." Then he ran over and tugged at a big boar coon. "Come on. Let's get these varmints loaded."

One by one, we filled up the back of the truck with sleeping coons. Some of them were big old boars weighing fifty pounds, it seemed to me. There were a lot of females and young ones, too. It was some job getting them into the truck, but we got them all. I thought some of them were sleeping rather lightly.

"Let's get going before this stuff wears off," I said.

"All right, everybody get in," Hawk said. "One of you better ride in the back with these critters."

"You do it, Barney. You're the oldest," Jake said, as he usually did when there was a dirty job to be done.

I piled in the back, and Hawk slammed the tailgate shut. "You sing out if you need anything, Barney," he said. "I'll get there as fast as I can."

It was weird back there. The floor was so crowded I had to pile some of them up to keep from lying on them, and they smelled strong. Thirty-two of them were practically in my lap!

I knew as soon as we started off that I'd made a

terrible mistake. A leak in the exhaust system just about strangled me, not to mention the roaring that just about ruined my eardrums. Then Jake did what he always did—turned the radio up full blast!

I made the best of it, and we made pretty good time. But then I remembered that there was construction on Highway 7 going to Hot Springs. Hawk would have to make a long detour.

It got worse and worse in the bed of that truck. I almost got sick from the smell of corn and exhaust, and the racket was driving me crazy!

I pounded on the back of the cab, but the road was so bumpy Hawk couldn't hear it. I tried yelling, but of course, I couldn't drown out the radio. Then it happened.

Something bit me on the ear! Not hard, but enough to make me jump. Then a tiny hand touched my ankle.

"The coons are waking up!" I screamed. I beat on the back of the cab as hard as I could and screamed like a baboon, but it was no use.

The coons were all over me. Coons usually aren't mean, but a big boar can tear a sixty-pound foxhound to shreds. My situation was dangerous.

But coons are the most curious animals in the world. A friend of mine left a baby coon in the bathroom for about an hour. That coon opened the medicine cabinet, opened every bottle, turned on every tap, unrolled all the toilet paper, unscrewed the light bulb, and generally wrecked the place!

These coons were curious about *me!* By the time we got where we'd agreed to turn them loose, I was nearly batty. They were pulling at my clothes, untying my shoes, trying to poke under my eyelids.

Finally we stopped. Hawk opened the tailgate and then was just about trampled by coons as they went for the open space. After they left, some of them still pretty wobbly from the tranquilizer, I crawled out fighting a strong desire to strangle Jake.

"Why, they woke up, didn't they!" Jake said in surprise. "Why didn't you let us know, Barney?"

I hated to tell him I'd suffered, so I just said, "Oh, it was *fun,* Jake. More fun than a barrel of monkeys! Next time *you* can ride with them!"

Jake grinned. "Naw, you're the oldest, Barney!"

8

Flight of the Solarcycle

AFTER we bought the solar cells, it took Joe another three days to mount them. Jake and I helped, and on Saturday the Solarcycle was ready.

We wheeled it out. Suddenly, the whole contraption seemed silly! A bunch of plastic bags and some fragile aluminum framing—I was going to trust my life to a thing like that?

Jake repeated his famous line, "You're the oldest."

But the longer I looked at the thing, the more I got a hollow feeling in my stomach.

"It can't miss, Barney," Jake said with a confident smile. "I personally guarantee it!"

"You would have guaranteed the *Titanic!*"

"They didn't have me around to take care of things," he said. "Now go on. We've got to get this thing in the air."

I crawled onto the seat.

Joe was as nervous as a hen with one chick. "Now don't go too high, Barney. I don't know if the gas bags will take a real high altitude. They might break—and that would be bad."

"Oh, I'd merely fall like a rock, Joe," I said grimly. "Well, here goes. You guys stand back."

I opened the valve in front of me, and a hissing sound escaped as the helium rushed along the tubing. The cigar-shaped bag began swelling and straining at the cords that held it. Then suddenly, before I was ready, the Solarcycle lurched up, and my stomach lurched along with it.

"Not too much gas—you'll bust the balloon!" Joe yelled.

I eased up on the gas. I was slowly rising. When I cleared the top of the barn, I looked down. It was scary. A little puff of wind caused the Solarcycle to nose down. I thought I was going to get dumped right on top of Joe and Jake, who already looked very small.

"More gas in the afterchamber!" Joe yelled.

I touched a little valve that allowed the front section to catch up. There were five sections, and I could send gas to any one of them.

I leveled off and looked down. I could see in every direction now—behind the house to the watermelon patch, out to the highway, where an old pickup was wobbling along, over by the creek, where a deer lifted his head to look up at me.

Jake and Joe were yelling, but I couldn't make out what they were saying. I was just drifting along, enjoying the view, when I realized I was being carried sideways by the breeze. With a start, I pushed a lever forward to activate the battery fed by the solar cells. Glancing back, I saw the prop start up, and then the cycle moved forward like it was supposed to. I caught my first thermal then—a warm breeze coming off a meadow that lifted me up. It worked! The Solarcycle worked!

I waved at Joe and Jake, who looked like toys far below. Then I turned the tiller, a set of handlebars from an old bicycle, and felt the machine answer at once. It was the most fun thing I'd ever done. I'd always been a little afraid of high places, but I felt safe.

To go higher, all I had to do was catch an updraft or let more gas into the chambers. I could go down by tilting the handlebar down or by letting the helium out of the gas bag. I could go forward by activating the prop. To turn right or left, I just had to turn the handlebars.

Instead of going back to Joe and Jake, I soared over Cedarville and spotted the school with all the yellow buses lined up in a row. I swooped down over the new Wal-Mart with its parking lot filled.

Nobody looked up, except one little kid, and he just stared. Cruising above town, I got a big kick out of seeing kids I knew fooling around in their yards. I wondered what they would think if I swooped down and yelled, "Boo!" at them. But that would have been too tricky to attempt. Besides, I didn't want anyone to know about the Solarcycle until later.

I made a slow turn, gained altitude, and headed for Panther Gap. It took only fifteen minutes of gliding along on the breeze, which was cold as ice, but I didn't care!

Then I saw the Leatherwood house. It looked just as pretty from the air as it did from the ground. Best of all, I saw Hawk and Robin in the backyard, hanging their wash on a line.

I couldn't resist. I pulled open the valve that released the gas from the chambers and maneuvered the craft right over their backyard, regulating the gas so that I hovered down almost on top of them. When I was about fifty feet away, I yelled, "Look out below! Here comes Barney Buck and the Flying Solarcycle!"

Well, I nearly scared both of them to death. They both jumped, giving me wild, staring looks with the biggest eyes I ever saw.

I was sorry, but now I had my hands full getting the

Solarcycle down without wrecking it. I did pretty well, and when I landed, the only damage I'd done was bend the tubing. Then the breeze caught the cycle and carried it along the ground toward the woods.

"Help me hold it!" I hollered.

Hawk and Robin came out of their shock, and the three of us stopped it. By that time, Mr. and Mrs. Leatherwood had come out of the house and were staring at the Solarcycle as though it had come from the moon.

"It's Joe's new invention!" I said. Then I gave them the good news. "It's going to catch the tree rustlers!"

It took awhile for me to convince them.

"See, I can drift around, no noise at all, and cover the whole county in one flight. I can see if anyone's at the trees. Then we can get word to the sheriff and—well, that's it!"

"But—is that thing safe?" Mrs. Leatherwood asked. "It looks so flimsy!"

I assured her it was safe, and then said, "I have to go. Joe and Jake are probably crazy by now. But we'll catch those tree rustlers. You'll see!"

I climbed onto the Solarcycle and got it ready to fly. It was so easy, now that I'd done it once. I took off like a big bird, turned the Solarcycle in a wide curve, and flew to Goober Holler with a wave of my hand.

Joe and Jake were still there, staring up. When I

landed, they both pitched into me for being gone so long.

"You could've been blown away to the ocean!" Jake fussed. "And I've got a third interest in that machine!"

"I was *worried,*" Joe said, getting close to me.

"I'm sorry, guys. It just got out of hand. Joe, you're a genius. The Solarcycle is a fantastic success!"

I told them all about my flight. Jake said he might like to try it, but actually both the boys were terrified of heights. Joe had gotten his fun building it, and Jake was planning to make a million dollars out of it. I was the pilot.

That day we started running the routes—or I did. I had maps, and it was so easy finding the places! I missed some of them, but for the most part, I had good luck. Nearly all the Leatherwoods' walnut trees were in the middle of pine forests owned by big timber companies, and since all his trees were bare this time of year, it wasn't hard.

When I got back, I told the Leatherwoods. "It's going to be easy! Even when I'm in school, most of the time I'll get home early enough to run half the route. Then I can check the other half the next day."

"Dad, can I go up in the Solarcycle?" Hawk said.

Mr. Leatherwood shook his head. "Son, I don't want you to do that—and neither does your mother. We knew you'd ask, and we have to say no." Hawk took it pretty well—better than I would have, I think.

Every afternoon I'd rush home from school and go up in the Solarcycle to check the trees. I didn't know why, but there hadn't been any trees taken for over a week. Still, it was a pretty safe bet there would be more stealing!

All this time, I was worrying about Debra. She was spending too much time with Rafe. Although we hadn't said a word since the fight, I felt like it wasn't over. Finally, I went to Coach Littlejohn and asked him what to do.

"I think you ought to go talk to her, Barney. It's all a misunderstanding, and you can't make it right without talking about it."

I was feeling pretty important—pilot of a plane and all—so I decided he was right. I would give her a break.

The next Friday afternoon, I went over to her house to invite her to a picnic. Cedarville had their big Winter Picnic every year, and it was considered a pretty important event. There were a lot of craft shows and concessions. I think it was put on to break the monotony of winter and to show it didn't have to be summer to be picnic time. There would be a big barbecue inside the pavilion at the fairgrounds.

I always got a little shaky when I went to the Simmonses' house. They were real well-off, and I felt a little like a beggar whenever I went up to the fancy front porch with the big white pillars. But I rang the bell, and Debra answered the door.

"Why . . . why, Barney . . . ," she stammered. Then I looked over her shoulder. There was Rafe with a big mug of cocoa in his hand.

He looked at me with a wide grin. "Come on in, killer. Me and Debra was just wondering whatever happened to you."

If I had my life to live over, I would have smiled at Rafe, gone right on in, and asked Debra to go to the picnic.

But I didn't. I just glared at Rafe and snapped at Debra. "I want to see your dad—about a dog."

"He . . . he's not here right now, Barney," Debra said. She looked real nervous, trying to watch me and Rafe at the same time, and I guess she was in a pretty tight spot.

"Well, I'll call next time before I come. Tell him I came by, will you?"

I stomped off down the porch, and Debra said in a very small voice, "I'll tell him, Barney."

Then Rafe said, "Come on in, honey. It's too cold out there for a pretty thing like you."

I walked all the way home and didn't even feel the cold. I decided I didn't want to go to a dumb old picnic anyway!

9
Mission in the Sky

YOU mean you're not going to the county picnic, Barney?" Robin asked. She'd stopped by with Hawk on the way to the fairgrounds, and I could tell she was disappointed.

"I'd like to, Robin, but I really need to make one more flight to that section over by Friendship. I haven't been there in three days, and that would be a likely place for the tree rustlers to hit. Your dad says it's the best stand of walnuts he has."

"I wish you could come. It won't be much fun without you." Robin had a way of pouting that almost made me say yes. But I was still sulking over Debra and Rafe, so I acted like a baby and decided not to go. That would show them! I knew I was cutting off my nose to spite my face, but I did it anyway.

All morning I messed around with Tim in the woods and pretty well managed to forget it. When Tim and I were out together, it wasn't hard for me to just enjoy the early December woods and let the rest of the world go by.

Finally at about one o'clock we came home with a couple of fat rabbits I'd picked off with the .22. I was skinning them for supper when I heard a truck roaring full speed down our road. Nobody would be driving that fast unless something was wrong. I got up and ran to the front yard to see what was up.

Hawk entered the clearing, the Dodge pickup swaying in the winter ruts, and slammed on the brakes so hard I thought Jake, who was beside him, would go right through the windshield!

"What's the matter?" I yelled. "Is Joe hurt?"

They both started yelling and pulling at me at the same time. I didn't understand a word except "balloon" and "Tad" and "lost."

"Wait a minute!" I shouted. "I can't understand you both. Hawk, what's wrong?"

He caught his breath, then said as quickly as he could, "Barney, you got to do something. Tad's lost. The balloon's busted loose and you've got to go after him!"

"What? I don't know what you're talking about!"

Jake broke in, his face pale. "Barney, I made a balloon like I saw in the paper. And I was letting kids go up for fifty cents, but it got away! The cord broke—and Tad Darrow is gonna get killed if you don't go get him!"

"Get him? Where is he? How can I get him?"

"There's no time to explain!" Jake said. His lips were trembling and he could hardly talk. "You . . . you got to get in the Solarcycle and bring . . . bring him down—with this!" He handed me his Daisy BB gun, and I took it.

"Get going, Barney!" Hawk said. "I'll fill you in while you're getting ready."

We ran over to the barn. As we pulled the Solarcycle out and I strapped myself into the seat, Hawk told me about it.

"Jake saw a story in the *Arkansas Gazette* about a fellow somewhere out east who took a bunch of weather balloons and tied them to a lawn chair. He just filled the balloons with helium and got onto the chair, and off he went."

"Hey, I saw that on TV!" I said. "He came down by shooting the balloons one at a time, so he came down easy."

"That's right," Jake spoke up, "but I just put the chair on a long rope, tied a bunch of balloons to it, and then fixed a winch on the old picnic stand. That way we could just let the kids go up a little way and then haul 'em down."

"That's right, Barney," Hawk agreed. He began checking the strap that held me on the Solarcycle. "Well, they only went up about thirty feet, and it was a lot of fun. But then Tad got in—and I don't know how it happened. Either the rope broke, or it wasn't tied to the winch. Anyway, it came loose, and the blamed thing went up like . . . like a balloon!"

"You gotta get him down, Barney!" Jake said in a quavering voice. "You gotta find him and shoot those balloons one at a time, or he'll die!"

"OK. Now you two get back and have Chief Tanner put this on the radio. Tell people to watch for Tad. Then when they see me in the Solarcycle, have them point the way he drifted. Got it? Stand back. I gotta get there quick."

I had charged the helium tank the day before, so it was full. What worried me was the stiff breeze coming out of the east. It was a cloudless day and the sun was shining, but a wind like that could blow Tad almost *anywhere.* He might come down hurt somewhere in the Ozark National Forest. We'd have some time finding him then!

I cleared the yard and waved at Jake and Hawk. They raced back to the truck, and I saw them rattle back down the road and turn on the highway toward the fairgrounds.

I got to the fairgrounds before they did. People were

milling around like ants. A few people had heard about the Solarcycle, but not many, so when I dropped out of the sky, some began yelling and screaming. They were all pointing up at me and I couldn't make any sense of it.

I spotted Chief Tanner, then did a turn and dropped down close enough for him to see it was me. I waved at him, but he just stared.

"Which way did he go?" I hollered as loudly as I could and made a sign with my hand around the sky. He got it right away and pointed almost due west, over toward Panther Gap. I waved at him, nosed the ship up, and gave it full power. The little propeller began humming, and I pedaled as hard as I could to gain a little speed. There was a lot of lift since I was heading into the wind, but it drove me up and I had to struggle not to go too high.

I figured Tad had been drifting for at least thirty minutes by now, and he could have gone in just about any westerly direction. I drove the cycle straight at first, but then I figured he might've drifted off. If I missed him, it could be really bad.

I did miss him, because after about thirty minutes I'd gone clear over the mountain at Panther Gap, and I knew he couldn't have drifted farther than that.

Somehow he'd gone either north or south, and I had no idea which way. *If I go north a little way, swing and go south, all the time heading back east, that'll be my best chance,* I thought. Once I read that was what the old sailing ships had done—tacking against the wind. I did that for the next hour.

After much time and effort I still hadn't found him. I felt sick. Maybe I hadn't gone far enough west and Tad was clear out of my range somewhere over the Ozarks. The poor kid must be scared to death!

I made a turn and headed west again. Then I heard something. *Blam! Blam! Blam!* At first I thought someone was shooting at me. I looked down and saw somebody standing in the middle of a huge field, waving a big piece of white cloth in one hand and letting go with a shotgun in the other. The man was trying to catch my attention.

"Hey!" I shouted. "Here I come!" I peeled off in a short wingover and made a dive right at him. I'd gotten pretty good with the Solarcycle. I sailed down not fifty feet over the guy. Then I realized it was Uncle Dave! His Jeep was parked at the edge of the field. Perhaps he'd heard the broadcast and had seen Tad.

"Hi, Uncle Dave!" I shouted as I approached him. "Have you seen Tad?"

I banked a little to see him. He dropped the cloth and the gun, cupping his hands over his mouth to shout, "He went by here about half an hour ago, Barney! Headed north by northwest!" He pointed toward the foothills lying to my left. "Go get him, boy!" I gave him a wave, then headed for the hills. I had to get Tad this time. I saw by looking down that nobody was going to give me any more help. The Ozarks are a thick national forest, where nobody lives! There were just a few tough campers this time of the year, but they wouldn't be listening to the radio.

I had one of my quick prayer times. Then it occurred to me that the times I really prayed were when I was in a mess! I thought about promising God to do better, but I didn't. I decided I'd try to stay "prayed up," as Uncle Dave put it, so that when the tough times came rolling around, I wouldn't be caught short.

The Lord must've given me credit, because I spotted the balloons five minutes later. I was pretty well over the Caddo River basin when I caught a glimpse of something red. I turned the cycle, and there he was—a lot higher than I'd thought. It was a wonder I hadn't missed him.

I climbed up. The air was cold enough to freeze spit, but I didn't care because as I swung around to get close, I caught a glimpse of Tad's terrified face. He saw me, and I thought he'd fall out of the flimsy lawn chair he was in.

"Help! Help!" he yelled.

"Sit down, Tad!" I shouted. "I'm going to get you down, but you have to be still and do just what I tell you, OK?"

He was a pretty good kid, that Tad Darrow. The Darrows were a rough bunch, but they had plenty of nerve! He'd been in the corral the day Rafe and I had fought, but I guess he saw I was his best bet right now.

"I got to find a good place to let you down, Tad," I called. "You might get hurt if you go down in those big trees." It looked like a solid forest as far as I could see in the direction he was headed. He didn't seem to be going any higher, so I made a few easy circles around him, being careful not to get too close. I pulled out the BB gun, tied the leather thong around the stock, and fastened the other end to the frame. If I lost the thong, it would be hopeless.

Then I saw a big open space, sort of a valley with grass instead of trees. Tad was going to pass right over it!

I hadn't figured out how to shoot the gun and fly the Solarcycle at the same time, but I had to do it right away, or we'd go beyond the valley.

"Tad, I'm going to shoot one of the balloons; so don't be scared!" I called out.

I climbed above Tad and put the Solarcycle into a slow turn. The balloons were about seventy feet away. There must have been thirty of them. I had no idea how tough they were, or how many I'd have to shoot to get the thing down.

It would be dangerous to let the handlebar control go—no telling what the Solarcycle would do. I leaned back and put my feet on the handlebars—just the way I'd done many times when riding a bicycle on the ground. Then I took the BB gun in both hands, drew a quick bead, and *plunk*—one of the balloons popped.

"You got it, Barney!" Tad shouted. "You done it!"

"Keep still, Tad," I called out. "I'll take them out one at a time, and we'll get you down light as a feather!"

That was the way it happened. I took out four more before it had any effect. Then, as I popped the fifth one, the whole thing settled a little and Tad gave a cheer. It was really easy. The meadow was level as a table, and I kept shooting the balloons until the whole thing floated down and set Tad down as easy as you please! I let out a deep sigh of relief.

Now I had to decide what to do with Tad. We were miles away from anything, and I couldn't leave him alone while I went for help. He was only seven. A kid like that would go bananas all by himself in the woods!

Finally, I did the only thing I *could* do. I set the Solarcycle down in the meadow, strapped Tad on in the back of my seat, and headed for the fairgrounds.

Tad was still pale, but he talked all the way there. When we finally saw Cedarville, he wiggled so much I had to settle him down. "Sit still, Tad. You'll fall out!"

It looked to me like everybody with a radio had come to the fairgrounds. They were all milling around, and even the fire truck was there. What for, nobody really knew.

Then they spotted us, and the band started playing! They'd been there to play for the picnic, and as I brought the Solarcycle in for a perfect landing, they struck up "Dixie"! The crowd went wild. They swarmed onto the field, picked us up, and rode me and Tad around on their shoulders while everybody cheered!

I was afraid they'd wreck the Solarcycle. Besides, I felt pretty silly up there! Finally they put us down, and I noticed Mort Darrow and a little woman with white hair I guessed was Tad's mother. They made a grab at Tad, and then the blubbering started.

"Barney! You're a hero!" Joe shouted.

"You want my autograph?" I said, giving him a quick rub on the head. "You're the hero! It's your invention."

Well, everybody quieted down, and then a funny thing happened. The crowd broke apart, and there I was facing the whole Darrow clan—at least twenty of them. I guess everybody was waiting for them to thank me or something.

The crowd was disappointed, though, because the Darrows took one look at me, turned, and went on home, Mrs. Darrow holding Tad in her arms. Rafe passed within five feet of me. He gave me a straight stare, but his mouth was shut tight and he didn't say a word. I figured the Darrows held a huge grudge against me for staying on Cyclone.

As they filed out, I heard people muttering, "Ungrateful whelps!" I saw Debra standing by her father, watching Rafe leave. She gave me a quick glance, turned red, and wheeled to run off, following the Darrows.

Coach was standing there and hadn't missed any of it. He gave my arm a squeeze. "Don't worry about it, Barney. She'll wake up."

Then Jake—the architect of the whole mess—popped up. He marched straight up to me and said, "Too bad we didn't have some photographers here. It would have been good publicity for us when we start production. Well, back to the old drawing board!"

I couldn't teach that kid anything!

10

Barney Bites the Dust

BOY! Look at that expression on your face!" Hawk laughed, spreading the paper on the rug in front of me. "Looks like it ought to be on a post office wall with Wanted by FBI written under it."

Jake's wish for a photographer had come true, but not in the way he wanted it. Somehow my picture had gotten in *The Daily Siftings* the Monday after the picnic. Most people called the paper "The Daily Mistake," which pretty well described it. They spelled my name "Buch" and gave my age as thirty-one instead of thirteen.

The picture that went with the story was worse. They had snapped it as I was being carried on people's shoulders. I looked like a criminal who'd just been caught.

"He doesn't look like a criminal!" Robin said, leaning on my shoulder and peering at the picture.

"Well, I'm glad you don't agree with your numbskull brother!"

"Nooo!" she said thoughtfully. "But in those pants you look like you're smuggling rice out of China!"

"Aw, cut it out, will ya?" I said. "What good does it do to be a blasted hero when you get no respect from your friends?"

"You sure didn't get rich from the reward the Darrows gave you," Hawk said with a grin.

"Reward!" Robin snorted. "They didn't even say 'thank you'!"

"Well, in a way, I don't blame them," I said. "After all, it was my brother Jake who was responsible for the whole thing."

"They could've been nicer!" Robin said. "That Rafe! He's so good-looking and so . . . so . . ."

"Some people would say he's better looking than I am," I said.

"Those *eyes!*" Robin said, then giggled as I missed her with a back-handed swipe. "Do you have to go up in the Solarcycle this afternoon, Barney? You've been up every day for so long!"

"I'd better. Miss one time, and one of those expensive trees that's supposed to make you queen of the college world will get stolen."

They followed me out to the Solarcycle. I had flown it so much, I didn't give it any more thought than I would getting on my bicycle and riding down the road.

I had only one stand of trees to check, and it wasn't too far. "Only four big trees over by Friendship, but they're the best of the crop," Mr. Leatherwood had said. I turned the cycle and watched the Ouachita River wind along its banks like a sparkling whip. Even though it was still pretty cold, I could see a few johnboats drifting along with fishermen who were trying to get a bass or some crappies.

It was so sharp and clear, I could look north and see Mount Pinnacle over by Little Rock seventy miles away. The smoke from the paper mills in Pine Bluff was rising like clouds of steam. It looked pretty. Too bad it stank!

It didn't take me long to drift over Friendship, which nestled close to I-40. Then I banked west and was soon over the area where the walnut trees stood. The whole earth looked green below, and it wasn't hard to spot the hardwoods. Hawk and I had gone up to the top of one tree in every grove and tied a big white flag right at the top to make it easy to spot, but I really didn't need it at this location. The whole area was in pines, and the bare limbs of those walnuts stuck out like sore thumbs.

I guess I'd gotten pretty relaxed. Once I'd flown to the different sites a few times, the patrols got to be pretty routine. That was why I almost missed it.

I glanced down at the grove, and when I didn't see any activity, I turned and started for home. Then, just as I was wheeling due south, a flash of yellow caught my eye about two hundred yards away from the trees. I stretched my neck. A shiver went all over me that made me straighten up, sending the Solarcycle into a steep bank and a dive. Even as I dropped, I heard the whine of a chain saw splitting the cold air and saw a big loader and a log truck. I sailed over, and there they were—two guys cutting down a walnut tree!

That was when I got the shakes. About ten different plans flashed through my mind, most of them impossible. It was funny, but we hadn't even considered what I should do if I spotted the rustlers.

I considered making for home and calling the sheriff, but I knew that I didn't have time. By the time I got back with cops, the rustlers would be long gone. If only I had a short-range radio! I could call in the location, and it would be easy for the sheriff to surround them, cutting off the roads while I stayed up and spotted them.

But it was too late to pray about that!

I knew all at once what I had to do. I made a sharp turn and dropped the nose of the cycle sharper than I ever had. Once the tree got loaded, the rustlers could make seventy miles an hour on I-40, and I couldn't keep up with them. I would have to drop down and try to get close enough to identify them!

I didn't even like the thought of it, but it was all I could think of. Actually, the way those chain saws were snarling, they'd never hear me, and who ever looked up anyway?

I dropped until the tops of the big pines were just a few feet under me. Was that hairy! Then I was over the little clearing where the two men were working. I got a quick glimpse of them as I started my glide. They had shut off their saws. They both were wearing the typical lumberjack's garb—jeans, plaid shirts, and billed caps. I leaned over to get a look at their faces. Suddenly it went all wrong!

One of them started to wipe his face with a red bandana and looked right up at me. I heard him curse, and the other one looked too. Just as I passed over, they dove for the truck and yanked the door open.

I thought they were going to run for it, but was I wrong! I'd gotten just a hundred feet away when I heard a sound I'll never forget. *Spang! Spang!* Then a long, whistling *Wheeeeee!*

An aluminum support in front of my right hand suddenly separated, and part of the wiring that held the gas bag steady fell into my face. They were shooting at me with a high-powered hunting rifle!

My first impulse was to climb and get as high as I could, but suddenly I knew that would be the end of me. A good hunter could hit a deer on the run half a mile away. It would be no trick for that guy to knock me right out of the air if I got up to where he could get a clear shot. So I did just the opposite. I stayed as close to the treetops as I could, then started to bear left.

Spang! Spang! Spang! The slugs were whistling all around me. I flinched, but there was no place to go. Then I heard another kind of noise. *Bahong! Bahong!* I saw little holes appear in the gas bag over my head.

I guess they both ran out of ammo, and it was a good thing for me! They'd hit the gas bag—at least one compartment—and part of the controls were shot away. The handlebars were loose and floppy in my grip, and the Solarcycle wasn't responding. I pulled back to gain altitude, but instead of going up, I dipped down. If I hit the tops of the trees, those guys would do me in.

Somehow I did all the right things. By instinct, I opened the valve that pumped the gas into the compartments. The sagging air bag that was flopping in the breeze started to swell up, making the cycle level off. The bottom of the cycle brushed against the top of a big pine, but it soon gained a little altitude.

Then I heard the loader and the truck start up. Those rustlers would be long gone by the time anyone got here. I had another problem, too. The cycle was rising, but there wasn't much forward motion—just what the tailwind provided. I looked behind me and saw the reason. One of the slugs had clipped the electrical wire that brought the current from the solar cells to the battery that powered the propeller.

Great! I thought, *Now I can work myself to death pedaling home!* Actually, I was pretty happy to be alive. The rustlers hadn't been playing around back there. I could've been lying on the ground. I felt lucky, except that I didn't really think it was luck.

Coach had said there wasn't any such thing. His favorite verse in the Bible was in Romans—something about all things working together for good to those that love the Lord. I guess I'd heard him say that a million times, but as I pedaled like crazy, I really believed it for the first time!

Finally I got home and called Sheriff Richards. He was out, and even though the call was sent to him, I knew it was too late.

The sheriff and his brother came out and took me and the Leatherwoods to the location, but they wouldn't let us go up close.

"We want to check for footprints and make casts of the tires of the equipment."

We stood back and watched while they made plaster-of-Paris molds. While they were hardening, we looked all around for other evidence, but there wasn't anything.

"If they'd just left a can of oil or gas, we could get prints," Sheriff Richards groaned. "But they're too smart for that." He looked at me. "Barney, didn't you get a look at those guys? You were pretty close, you said."

I was real embarrassed. "I . . . I guess not. All I saw were two men wearing jeans and plaid shirts. I didn't get a look at their faces."

Sheriff Richards seemed pretty disgusted with me. He'd worked hard trying to get the rustlers, and now I'd blown the first lead! "But—what about their hair, anything like that?"

"They wore caps," I mumbled.

"Did you get the license number?"

"N-no . . ."

"Well, what kind of truck was it? And the loader, what make was it?"

"Gosh—I don't know, Sheriff! I just didn't have time. . . ."

He must've taken pity on me, because he grinned and gave me a pat on the shoulder. "Don't feel bad, Barney. After all, you've done more than anyone else. Maybe we'll get something from these treads."

"You really think so?" I asked.

He made a face and said sourly, "It would be a million-to-one shot. Most trucks use the same kind of tires, and these guys are *sharp*. They'll probably change all the tires on the equipment. Well, we'll get 'em. If you snuck up on 'em once, you can do it again. You just keep flying that contraption, Barney."

That was about it. It wasn't too hard to fix the Solar-cycle. I flew every day for a week but didn't see anything, and no more trees were taken.

"Maybe they're scared off," I said to Mr. Leatherwood one day.

He shook his head. "No. They're just laid back. They can wait. Greed isn't like a cold, Barney, that goes away."

He was right about that, because it was just three days later that he came over to our place with Hawk and Robin in the pickup. The look on his face spelled bad news.

"They got another one, Barney. I knew they wouldn't quit."

"Where was it?" I asked.

"One of those nice ones on the river bottom over close to Malvern."

I stared at him. "That's impossible, Mr. Leatherwood. When did you check it?"

"Why, we just came from there. The wood chips weren't even dry, so they must have gotten it no longer than a day or two ago."

My heart sank. I said slowly, "They got it no later than last night!"

"How you figure that?" he asked, but I think Hawk knew what I was going to say because he grimaced.

"They cut that tree after dark—sometime last night." I sat down on the steps feeling weak. "I flew over that tree about four o'clock yesterday afternoon. It was up then. So it must've been cut before dawn. That means they've figured out a way to keep me from catching them in the Solarcycle!"

He nodded. "Yes, they can take one a night easy. Which means we're helpless."

Hawk dug in the dust with his toe, and Robin watched me sadly.

Mr. Leatherwood turned to go, but just before he left, he said the only bitter thing I'd ever heard out of his mouth.

"I don't guess God figures we're worth bothering with, Barney. You might as well not waste your prayers on the Leatherwoods."

As they left, I wished I could think of something to say, but I couldn't think of a single thing.

11

Friendship Comes High

AFTER a week I quit the daylight patrols. It was pretty clear they were useless. During that time two more trees were taken at night.

Sheriff Richards stopped by late one afternoon. "Barney, keep this to yourself, but we may have a lead."

"You mean the tire tracks?"

"No, that didn't pan out. What we have is an eyewitness who puts some suspects in the area where you were shot at, and at the right time."

"Golly! Who is it?"

The sheriff shook his head. "I don't want this to get around, Barney, not yet. The thing is, I did some checking on the other thefts, and these same suspects were seen in at least three locations at the time the other trees were taken."

"Why don't you arrest them, sheriff?"

"Because I have no proof, and they're pretty slick customers, Barney. You know them."

"It was the Darrows, wasn't it, Sheriff Richards!"

He nodded, then said quickly, "Don't say a word about this, Barney. I'm going to put them under surveillance—especially at night. If they move one piece of their logging equipment, we'll get 'em! But not a word!"

I nearly spilled the beans, but I couldn't tell anyone—not even Hawk. I was so anxious to do something to show the Leatherwoods that God hadn't abandoned them!

It was another week before anything happened, and then I got a call from Mr. Leatherwood. "They got two more, Barney. I just called to tell you that I'm selling out next week. Thanks for all you've done, but it's no use." He hung up.

As quickly as I could, I called Sheriff Richards.

Right away he said, "Barney, it didn't work—what we were talking about. Do you know how many trucks that man has? Nine! I can't watch all of them, and they're scattered all over creation! Until I can get more men, we're whipped!"

"Yeah, I guess you're right, Sheriff. So long."

For three days I walked around like a dead man or

something. Joe and Jake knew what was bothering me, but they couldn't say much to cheer me up.

It was awful with Robin and Hawk. We tried to joke and have a good time when we were together, but it wasn't any good. Robin and I even had a fuss—over Rafe Darrow!

I was on my way to English class, and there they were, walking together big as you please! I wondered where Debra was, since she usually clung to Rafe. My next thought was that Robin ought to be whipped after all that turkey had said about her and her family.

I grabbed her arm and said, "Come on, Robin. We got things to talk about!" Rafe just shrugged and moved on. I bawled her out. I told her how bad it looked for her to be seen talking to a Darrow—especially *that* Darrow! She just smiled up at me.

"But, Barney, we have to be nice to each other. Isn't that what they tell you at that church you go to?"

"Don't bring religion into this!" I said angrily. "You don't know what you're doing—just like Debra Simmons! Have you all gone nuts?"

Robin put her hand on my arm. "Barney, I know you don't like him, and maybe he's been wrong. But how can anyone change if he doesn't have somebody to help him?"

I saw it all then! Coach had said it—these nice young

girls wanted to reform the tough eggs like Rafe, but would wind up getting squashed.

"You just forget him, Robin!" I said loudly. When I was losing an argument, I always got louder. "We'll have no more of it!" But I knew that wasn't the end of it.

Just before supper, Joe called me away from my algebra book to come to his laboratory.

"Not now, Joe! I gotta try to understand this *mess!*"

"But, Barney, it's important!" Joe stood there, and like always I did what he wanted.

He led me out to the Solarcycle and waved a hand at it. "There, Barney, I got it all fixed."

"Fixed? What does that mean, Joe?" I hadn't ridden the thing for three days because there wasn't really any need. Joe had said he wanted to "modify" it.

"I mean, you can use it to get those ole tree rustlers, Barney."

I gave him a grin, then shrugged. "No use, Joe. They're cutting them at night."

"Sure, I know. That's what I've been doing. Look here," he said with a grin. He took me closer and touched some black cases strapped on with duct tape. "See these? They're batteries, Barney. They hold a charge. You can let them charge during the day and then run on them at night when the sun isn't shining.

"I got the idea from a movie I saw about submarines in World War II. They charged their batteries on the surface, then they went under and ran on them, and nobody could see them. Well, that's the way this works. You don't have to fly in daytime! Ain't it neat!"

It sure was! I thought again about how Mr. Addison had said Joe had the ability to take different things and put them together to make something new. He'd sure done it in this case, but it also meant I was in trouble.

I hadn't told a soul about it, but I'd never really gotten over that night I'd spent hanging on the ledge in the dark. I was less scared of high places now, and I wasn't afraid of the dark. But I was scared to death of being up high *and* in the dark at the same time!

I'd found that out while hunting at night. On the ground I was fine, no matter how dark it was. And during the day there wasn't a cliff I wouldn't tackle. But one night I tried to climb a pretty steep bluff where Tim was chasing a coon, and I'd gotten so scared I actually got sick!

From then on I just stayed in the low country at night. Most coons stayed in the bottoms anyway, so I figured it didn't make any difference.

Now it did. Joe's new wrinkle meant I could go up in the Solarcycle the darkest night there was and soar around a thousand feet in the air. It made my stomach ache even to think of it!

"Well, Joe, that's great, but there are lots of problems with flying at night—landing, for instance."

I thought I had him, but he nodded happily. "That's easy, Barney! I put lights out in a circle here. You know how to land the ole Solarcycle on a pin-head anyway!"

I talked as fast as I could, but every time I thought up a difficulty, Joe had an answer. Finally I couldn't think of any more reasons except that I was scared blue, but I didn't have the nerve to tell him that!

"Yeah, well, we'll certainly have to make some plans, won't we, Joe?" I knew he expected me to take off as soon as it was dark, but no way was I going to do that!

"But, Barney, we even have a two-way radio. See? I can sit here, and you can call right back as soon as you see anything."

"Joe, will you be quiet!" I shouted. "How would we know it was the rustler cutting down the tree? It could be anybody!"

Joe stared at me. "Barney, don't be dumb! What would an honest timber-cutter be doing a thing like that at night for?"

It was the only time in his life he'd ever been sharp like that to me, and what hurt was that I knew I'd forced him into it. Finally I just walked off and grumbled, "We'll have to make some plans."

I guess Mrs. Simpkins and Jake wondered what was wrong with me. We had Mexican food, which I usually could eat like crazy, but not that night. I muttered something about having an upset stomach, then went out for a walk.

Tim went with me, of course, and we went for a long walk that lasted nearly two hours. Most of the time I spent thinking how it wouldn't be sensible to go up in the Solarcycle at night. Or practical. Anyone with common sense—I stopped short.

Coach had said in Sunday school class, "I've noticed there's one phrase that always means the guy saying it is determined not to trust God. When you hear someone say 'Yes, but God gave us common sense,' don't look for that dude to have any faith! He's running on his own steam.

"Daniel could have said that, couldn't he? How much sense did crawling in with a bunch of hungry lions make? Noah could have said, 'God, it's not practical!' I'm telling you, fellas, there's going to be a time in the life of every one of you when common sense won't be worth a dime—only your faith to believe that God can do the impossible!"

I knew as sure as I stood there that God wanted me to go up in the Solarcycle! But I would've given anything on earth to have gotten out of it!

All the way back to the house, I tried to shake it off, telling myself it was just a crazy idea. God couldn't be in it at all. But I kept thinking of two things.

One was the part in *Huckleberry Finn* where Jim, the

runaway slave, runs into Huck at the river. My literature teacher, Mr. Burton, had said, "At that time the worst thing in the world for a white boy to do was to help a runaway slave escape to free territory. Huck thought if he helped Jim get away, he'd go straight to hell. All night long he struggled with it, then he decided to turn Jim in. But when Jim said, 'Huck, you is my only friend,' Huck just couldn't do it! Know what he did? He looked at Jim and said, 'All right! I'll just go to hell then, if that's what it takes to save Jim!'"

I never forgot that, or something else just like it—a verse out of the Bible: *Greater love hath no man than this, that a man lay down his life for his friends.*

By the time I got back to the house, I was still scared and worn out from fighting with myself, but I was ready to do what needed to be done.

"Joe, get your radio!" I yelled. "I'm going up!"

12
Night Flight

I didn't go up that night. We had run out of gas for the cycle. Hawk would have to take me to Hot Springs the next day to get a new tank.

Not going up right away led to a problem, though. I had all day to think about it and fall apart. By the time evening arrived, just the thought of climbing up into those dark clouds was enough to make me want to find a hole to crawl into. But as I was getting ready to explain why I wasn't going up, I had a visitor.

I was sitting on the porch listening to Jake and Joe work with the radio when I heard a truck coming. As it pulled into the yard, I saw it was Uncle Dave's.

Uncle Dave was pretty old, but he was the toughest

man in Goober Holler! He was Debra's granddad, and he'd been a help to us since we'd come to live in Goober Holler. If anyone could help me, he was the one. I ran over and pulled the door open.

"Uncle Dave, you have to help me out."

Suddenly somebody fell out of the pickup right into my arms. It sure wasn't Uncle Dave! He didn't have soft skin or smell as sweet as the one I stood there holding.

"Debra!" I said. "What in the world . . . ? I didn't know you could drive!"

"I can't!" she said. "But I had to come, Barney! I've been just miserable!"

"You have?"

"Yes! I think I must have lost my mind, Barney! Just went crazy!"

"Well . . . well . . ." I stood there stammering, and our faces were close enough so I could see her lips trembling. She looked ready to break down and cry.

"Aw, Debra, *I'm* the one who's been crazy. It's all my fault. I know that Rafe is ten times smarter and better looking than I am. . . ."

"You hush, Barney Buck!" she snapped, putting her soft hand over my mouth. "What in the world do I care about *him? I wish I'd never seen that big . . . hunk!"*

I pulled her hand away. "But I thought you . . . well, it *looked* like you liked him, Debra."

"Well, I don't."

She leaned against me, and my knees started to shake. My mouth went dry.

"Gosh, Debra, I'm sure glad to hear that. You know, I've always said we were the best of buddies, haven't I? And no two people could be better friends than us, could they?"

She tapped her lower lip with her finger. "Oh, sure, we're *good* friends, Barney."

Then that fool girl kissed me. Right on the lips! Boy, was I embarrassed. "Is that good enough *friends* for you, Barney Buck?" she said.

"Well . . . well, I guess it's sufficient, Debra!"

She laughed, and it was like old times.

Debra stayed until Joe and Jake hollered, "You can go anytime, Barney. Radio's checked."

"Go?" Debra said with a wrinkle on her brow. "Go where?"

"Well, I'm going to take the Solarcycle up for a flight." I explained why I had to do it, and she just stared at me.

"But you could get killed, Barney!"

"I sure could—and I really don't want to do it, but you see, Robin and Hawk saved my life. I've got to do it for them. You see that, don't you, Debra?"

I was half afraid she'd go off like a firecracker when I mentioned Robin, but she didn't. She just shook her head and said, "I don't want you to go up there, Barney."

"Well, *I* don't want to go either, Debra. Shoot! You

know all that hogwash they wrote in the *Siftings* about me being so 'brave' and a 'hero' and all that stuff? Why I'm not any of that. But I have to do it, even though I'm scared to death."

I thought she was about to walk off and leave me, which I wouldn't have blamed her for—me being such a coward and all. Instead, she smiled that good smile of hers and said, "I'm not so sure all that stuff about you was wrong, Barney."

"But I tell you I'm just about petrified, Debra!"

"But you're going, aren't you?" she asked.

I nodded.

"I'm glad I have you for a friend, Barney Buck," she said in a gentle tone, close to a whisper.

She said she'd stay with the boys and listen to the radio while I was up. I told her that there was another radio over at the Leatherwoods, so that if I was too far from one, the other ought to pick me up.

"Good-bye for a while," I said, trying to be brave. It wasn't easy to climb on that machine and lift off into the dark!

But once I was up, I was so busy I had to stop being scared a little just to take care of business. I'd done a little homework—getting all the locations clear in my mind and trying to think what to use for landmarks, maybe lights of some kind.

When I was up a few hundred feet, I looked around,

and it was a surprise how much light there really was! I could see the radio tower of KVRC blinking off and on, and there was Malvern just seventeen miles away lit up like a Christmas tree! There were houses everywhere, even in the timbered areas. It was surprising how much light they gave off.

I made a turn, went to my first checkpoint, and tried the radio. It was real simple and had a good range.

"This is Solarcycle to ground. Do you read me?"

"Jake to Solarcycle. We read you. How's it look, Barney?"

"Not too bad. I'm going to checkpoint one."

"Leatherwood to Solarcycle, do you read me?" It was Hawk's voice, a little faint because of the distance to Panther Gap, but otherwise sharp and clear.

"Solarcycle to Hawk. I read you clear. Headed for checkpoint one."

Hawk and Jake had maps. We'd marked the different stands and given them numbers. If I saw anything, they were to call the sheriff and get him on the way.

I felt like an actor in an old movie about World War II. There I was, Barney Buck, ace fighter pilot of the Hat-in-the-Ring Squadron, out to meet Baron von Richthofen in single combat over no man's land!

Actually, I got real tired. Going through the checkpoints took all my concentration, and I sure didn't want to get lost at night. I had to use the updrafts as much as possible because the batteries were limited. I did a lot of pedaling to save them, and I was worn to the bone.

Finally I was over the southernmost area.

"Solarcycle to Hawk. Approaching checkpoint seven."

"Hawk to Solarcycle. I read you. Do you see anything?"

"No, not a thing. Wait a minute!"

I took a hard look off to my left.

"Yes! I see some lights right about where the checkpoint is. I'll get closer."

"Hawk to Solarcycle. Be careful. Remember what happened last time!"

"Solarcycle to Hawk. It'd be hard for them to recognize me this time. Hawk, it's them! I can hear the saws! Call the sheriff and have him close off old Highway 9. They could leave that way!"

"Roger. Will do!"

I kept an altitude of about three hundred feet, but they were using heavy-duty flashlights and the lights of the vehicles to work by. I could see two men. Then I heard the saw stop and the crash of a big tree going down.

I got back to Hawk. "Hawk, a tree is down, and it won't take long to cut the limbs and load it. Is Sheriff Richards on his way?"

"Hawk to Solarcycle—no! Can't raise him, Barney. Look, I'm coming myself. We can't let them get away."

"You can't, Hawk! These guys are killers. You know how the whole county talks about the Darrows, how mean they are!"

"The Darrows?" Hawk asked. "Is that who you think it is? Well, Dad's here and we'll get some help. You stay up, and we'll take the radio so you can track them for us if they leave."

I tried to stop him, but he was off the air. He was crazy! Those guys would pick him off like a squirrel if they got a shot. All I could hope for now was that someone would get hold of the sheriff. I picked up Jake, and he said he'd keep trying to get him.

I sailed around for about five minutes. Then I noticed they were already pulling the loader into position! Those guys were fast! In another five minutes they had that tree chained down and were pulling out. I had no choice but to follow them.

They took an old logging road that I couldn't even *see.* I kept up with the headlights and tried to get Hawk, but couldn't.

I tracked the rustlers until they hit old Highway 23 to Prescott. They picked up speed as soon as they hit the blacktop road. I had been mostly pedaling, but now they were pulling away from me, so I turned on the prop switch. The Solarcycle leapt forward. I hoped the rustlers weren't going far, because I didn't think the batteries would last long.

Finally I got a call from Hawk and told him, "They're on Highway 23, moving fast. Wait, I think they're turning. Yeah, it must be an old logging road."

"Boy, can you see any landmark?"

I didn't recognize the voice, but I looked around and said, "They're turning right, beside some kind of a pool, a pretty big one, and there's some kind of tall white building on the highway."

"That's the old barpit and the grain dryer," the strange voice said. "Let's git. Barney, you keep it up!"

I didn't have much time to worry about who that was. My problem was the batteries. They were getting weaker. I'd drained them dry by leaving them wide open, but I'd had to keep the trucks in sight. Now I was slowing down and pedaling like mad to keep up, and the rustlers were still ahead of me and fast disappearing down a road.

"Hawk! I've got them. I've found their warehouse! It's a big tin building right in the middle of the woods, and the only landmark I can see is two little hills that stick up like—like pyramids on each side of it! I don't see—"

Crash!

I was so busy trying to look and talk and control the cycle, I didn't pay enough attention to how low I had gotten. Just as I hit, I saw the top of a massive pine, which seemed to reach out and grab the Solarcycle. I suddenly flipped upside down and started dropping through the top branches of the tree.

Well, I hope they get here! I thought. *Sure would hate to do all this for nothing. . . .* Then something hit me in the back of the head, and the world went black!

13

Wrong End of the Rope

I started to wake up, but my head hurt so bad, I tried to slide back into the nice, warm dark.

"Barney! Barney!" Somebody was calling my name, not very loud.

"Will you shut up and leave me alone!" I tried to shout, but all I could manage was a tiny whisper. I wondered what was wrong with my voice as I slid back into the dark.

"Barney? Where are you? Can you hear me?"

"Oh, for crying out loud! Leave me alone!"

But the voice kept on. "Barney, where are you? Are you hurt?"

Finally I opened my eyes, and that *really* made

my head ache. I was lying on my back looking up through the tops of tall trees. I saw part of the moon appear from behind a cloud and then heard the voice again.

"Barney, answer me!"

It was Debra, but where was she? I tried to move, but my right arm hurt so bad I had to grit my teeth to keep from crying. Then I heard my name again. I slowly sat up and noticed a small black object that had a tiny speck of light coming out of it. The short-wave radio! It hadn't been smashed when I fell!

I held my hurt arm with my free hand and managed to stagger over to where it was. Just moving made me dizzy. I had to sit down and lean against the tree before the world stopped spinning.

I managed to push the button and croaked out in a little voice, "This is Barney. Is that you Debra?"

"Barney! It's you! Oh, we've been *sick* thinking you crashed or something! Where are you?"

"Well, actually I don't know, Debra. I did crash, and my head feels bashed in so I can't stand up without falling down, and I think my arm is broken. As long as I hold it with my other hand, it's all right. Aside from that, I'm OK."

I heard her gasp. Then she said, "But, where are you, Barney? We heard you talking, and then you just were cut off."

"Debra, I don't *know.* But I'm not far from where the rustlers have stashed the trees."

Then I made the mistake of trying to stand up, and the world started spinning. I fell down again, right on my bad arm.

The pain was so awful I hollered, and then I passed out. When I came to again, I heard Debra's voice, but it sounded far off. Then I heard other voices, which I couldn't make sense of. Somebody was pulling at me, but I hurt too bad to care until he picked me up. The pain nearly killed me, and I managed to say, "Put me down! You're hurting me!"

"Kid's still alive," somebody said in surprise. "I thought he croaked in the crash!"

Then the one who was carrying me said, "Is he? Too bad."

Too bad! That told me everything. The thieves had me! That brought me to my senses.

I tried to get loose, but the one carrying me laughed and said, "Wiggle all you want to, kid. You won't be wiggling long."

I struggled harder and started shouting, "Let me go! The police are on the way! You can't get away!"

Both of them laughed. Then I was set down hard and fast.

"I guess you're able to walk. It's not far," said the one who had been carrying me.

The moon was getting clear of the clouds. I looked at the rustler and caught my breath.

"Sheriff Richards!"

"And my deputy! Surprised, aren't you, Barney!"

Thad Richards was dressed in logger's clothes, and so was his brother, R.D. They stood there grinning at me, but I just couldn't believe it!

"I thought you said . . ."

Then I realized what we should have known all the time. The rustlers always knew when they'd been spotted because we'd almost always told the sheriff.

"I got a big kick out of investigating that truck-tire print, kid. Looking for my own fingerprints on a can I knew we hadn't left! We had to scurry around a bit to get rid of some of the real clues we left behind, didn't we, R.D.?"

"I even left my cant hook with my initials on it there. Had to pick it up while you were messing with that plaster stuff."

"Well, let's get going," Thad Richards said, a mean look covering his face.

"What . . . what are you going to do to me?" I asked, trying to keep my voice steady. "I radioed your location. Somebody is coming."

R.D. patted his rifle and said, "If they do, it'll be just too bad."

"But the police . . ."

"Barney, we *are* the police!" Thad Richards said with a harsh laugh. "You forget that?" He pulled me down the trail.

"But they'll know about you!" I said.

"No, they're too dumb." R.D. laughed. "We'll see how it goes. If it's somebody we can't handle, we'll just tell him we picked up the message on our radio and got here just a few minutes before the crooks knocked you on the head."

So, that's what they're going to do to me! I thought.

"If it's just punks, we'll let them have it and lay it on the bad old tree rustlers. Who's gonna know?"

Nobody. I cried out again as they pulled me. I had no chance at all. They held me tight and dragged me down the path. I tried to think of something to do, but it was no use. I guess I was afraid, but mostly I was sorry I wouldn't be able to do all the things I'd planned—like going to Little Rock for Jake's concert and entering Tim in the state field trials for coon-hounds—just little things. I realized as we headed toward an open area that those little things were what really mattered. If I'd known that before now, I would have done more of them.

We stopped beside a big hole in the ground. I looked down and saw the gleam of the moon on the water, and I knew it was a barpit—one of the deep holes made in mining for bauxite. When a hole fills up with rain, it's good for swimming in—sometimes fifty or a hundred feet deep.

R.D. was doing something to my leg. I looked down and saw he'd tied a sledgehammer head to it with a piece of rope.

"Don't reckon you could swim long with a broken wing, but *that* settles it."

Thad Richards took me by the shoulders and stood right behind me. I looked down into the dark water and thought that, of all the times in my life to be afraid, this ought to be the worst time of all.

But I just wasn't. I don't really know why.

"Kid, I don't want to do this," Thad said suddenly. "But you ain't left me no choice. I couldn't stand the pen and neither could R.D. We been outdoors all our lives, and we'd go nuts in there. You . . ." He cleared his throat and said, "You wanna say anything—like maybe a last prayer or something?"

I guess he was working himself up to it.

I said, "No. I guess all I can say to both of you is this: Awhile back I gave my life to Christ. I never thought a thing like this could happen to me, but right now, I'm mighty glad I did that. And I'm sorry for both of you."

"Get it done!" R.D. said harshly. Thad's hands tightened on my shoulders.

"Hold it, Richards!"

Thad gave a jerk and turned me loose. I knew he was trying for the gun on his hip, just as R.D. was, but then a light shot out and caught the three of us in a powerful beam.

The strange voice said, "Don't move a muscle, either of you! I got a thirty-thirty trained right between your eyes, Thad! You move one finger and you won't have to worry about lawyers and trials and such!"

"You can't get both of us!" R.D. shouted. Then just as he reached for his handgun, another light went on about twenty feet to the left of the first one.

"You just reach for it, R.D.," another voice said. "I sure would love for you to give me the excuse to drill you right where you stand!"

Three more lights went on, and the first voice said, "You two freeze. Somebody go get their guns while the rest of us hold 'em on a point!"

Hawk came out of the darkness, plucked the two guns from the two Richards brothers, then put his arm around me. If he hadn't, I would have fallen over backwards into the barpit. That would have been a mess—drowning after they'd saved my life! Just the sort of dumb thing I'd do!

"Hawk, I didn't think you'd make it," I said as he knelt and untied the hammer head.

"I wouldn't have if it hadn't been for these guys," he said. The lights bobbed closer.

"Gosh, I don't know who you are, but I sure do thank—" I began.

"Don't know who we are!" the voice I'd heard over the radio said. "I'm the old geezer you done out of five hundred hard-earned dollars, boy. That's who I am! Don't you tell me you don't know *me!"*

"Mr. Darrow!" I gulped. And then I saw another one beside him that I couldn't believe. "Rafe, you . . ." Then I just couldn't think of a single thing to say, except to tell the truth. "Well . . ."

Rafe just grinned and stuck his hand out. "I got a pretty good idea what you thought, Barney. We may be a pretty wild crew, but we ain't thieves."

"Now, boy, this about squares us, don't you think?" Mr. Darrow asked. "I mean, you saved Tad—now we've saved you. Are we even?"

"Sure, Mr. Darrow!" I said.

He frowned at me and said fiercely, "Well, you just watch out for yourself, you hear? Us Darrows pay our debts, and I figure we paid up in full tonight. So you're on your own when it comes to dealing with us Darrows, boy!"

He sounded mean, but I saw Rafe wink at me like he was tickled.

"We better get you back to town, Barney," Rafe said. "Get that arm fixed. That little ole girl you been worried about, why she about drove us nuts as we were coming over here. I swear, you wouldn't *believe* what that Debra Simmons swore she'd do to me if I let you get killed! Where you reckon a nice young lady learned to talk like that, Pa?"

Well, they took us all in, and when we got to town, Chief Tanner said to the two prisoners, "You boys better take a look around—outside here. You ain't gonna see it again till you're old and gray-headed."

He herded them off to their cells, and the Darrows took me to the hospital. It was the middle of the night, but practically everybody I knew was there.

The emergency room was packed! Jake and Joe were hollering and trying to hug me. Coach Littlejohn, several of the teachers, Uncle Dave, the whole Simmons family, the basketball team—everybody, it looked like.

They were all laughing and trying to talk to me. Finally Doc Adams said, "Git the whole crew outside! Nurse, throw all these people out!"

And she did—all but one. As they got me onto the table and were about to slip an oxygen mask over my face, I heard the same voice I'd heard over the radio when I'd crashed. "Barney? I'm here." A soft hand found mine, and I let her hold it till I passed out.

You have to put up with a *lot* from girls sometimes!

14

The World's Greatest Singing Group

A few days after all the tree rustling excitement was over, Mr. Leatherwood stopped by the hospital. "How's the arm, Barney?"

"Oh, it's fine. Look at all the cards I got."

He stared around the room. "Looks like everybody in the county sent you one. Well, I just wanted to stop by and tell you about the timber."

"Was it in that big shed like we thought?"

"Every stick of it!" he said with a grin. "And it was all done right, too. Those boys could've made a good living as lumbermen if they hadn't been so crooked! Well, I've had it sent to the mill. Then it goes to the kiln dryer."

He pulled a sheet of paper out of his pocket and handed it to me. "Here's the bid I got on what was in the shed, not counting the trees still not cut."

He laughed when I made a gulping noise and my eyes popped out.

"Gosh," I said, handing it back to him. "If that Hawk is too dumb to make it through any college you pick out, why you can just buy the blamed school and make him president!"

He smiled, then got serious and put his hand on my shoulder. "It's all your doing, Barney. If you and Joe and Jake hadn't been around, that pair would have bled me white! Now you listen, and don't give me any static. Part of this is yours."

I started to protest, but he stopped me.

"Hush for a change!" Then he grinned and said, "I ain't noticed the Buck boys are very good at hushing! Anyway, there's going to come a time when you'll want to go to college yourself. And Jake—if he stays out of trouble with those schemes of his—he'll sure want to go. And Joe, well, he's special, Barney. But I don't have to tell you that. Now, I've set up a trust fund for the three of you. It's not enough to do everything, but it'll draw interest until you're ready. So don't argue with me about it."

I gulped and said, "Well, we sure thank you, Mr. Leatherwood. And I'm real happy for Hawk and Robin."

He looked a little uncomfortable, but finally said, "One more thing, Barney. About that prayer you made for us. I've never had any time for the Lord. I know I should have, not just for the family, but for me. Well, Teena and I had a long talk about how you trusted God to come through for the Leatherwoods and he did! I just want you to know that I ain't going to forget it. It's going to be different for the Leatherwoods from now on."

He gave me a good shake with his rugged hand, and I knew that something good had happened to him and his wife!

He got up and said, "They're telling me you're going to get out of here in time to make that fool concert in Little Rock. That so?"

I made a face. "I guess so. If a member of your family is bound and determined to disgrace the rest of you, why, the least you can do is be there to help pick up the pieces."

I got out of the hospital the next day, and it was only a week later that Joe and I got onto the school bus with a whole bunch of crazy kids. Jake had convinced them that this group, which he now called "The Termites," was going to win that big first prize.

I sat by Debra, of course, and we had a good time laughing at Jake's ambitions.

"He doesn't realize that he'll be competing with

groups lots older and with musicians that have played for years—some of them for money."

Debra laughed. "Let him have it his way, Barney. Even when he loses, it'll be something for him to remember."

"Yeah, I guess, but he scares me."

Debra looked around the bus. "I don't see the Leatherwoods. Aren't they going to be there?"

"Oh, sure, but they said they'd go in the car," I said.

I was proud of Debra. After she'd gotten the fool notion about Robin and me out of her head she'd become good friends with her. They began going places together, and that was good to see. Some people said it was just because Robin had come into money, but I knew that wasn't so.

We got off at the Robinson Auditorium, which was packed with about ten million idiots yelling their heads off! It was like a little war just getting to our seats.

When the show started, I sat there wondering how anybody could make any sense out of the music.

"What are they *saying?"* I asked Debra more than once. "I can't understand a word."

She leaned toward me and hollered over the noise, "They're saying, 'Ooo-ooo-ahhh-ahhh bay-beeeee bay-beeeee!' I'm surprised you don't grasp the depth and meaning of these words, Barney," she said with a laugh.

Joe was sitting right by me, enjoying it all. He'd

already forgotten the Solarcycle and was trying to make a machine that would keep cows in a pasture without a fence—by putting a radio in their ear or something. He'd probably do it, too!

Finally Jake and The Termites came out wearing sequined overalls. I had to admit they looked pretty good!

Jake had more poise than an undertaker! He took over and they played two songs. I didn't understand them any more than the rest of the stuff I'd heard. Then they played their own special number. The one Jake had written for the contest.

He stood up and just waited until the whole place got quiet—which was no little trick in itself! Then he said in a clear voice, "We will now play the song I have written especially for this contest. I respectfully suggest that you listen to the words of this wonderful song—about *Mother!!*"

I nearly fell out of my chair! "Is he crazy?" I whispered to Debra. "This bunch doesn't want to hear about *Mother!* They want to hear about my bay-beeeee done me wrong! That kind of stuff."

"I dunno, Barney," Debra said with a twinkle in her eye. "Maybe a change of pace will catch them off guard."

After a few rolls of the drum, the bass picked up a beat. Then the lead guitar, a skinny freshman named Kent Bible let the melody fall into place, and it wasn't too bad! I was shocked to discover that Jake even knew what a melody was, much less that he could actually write one! Then they all got with it, playing it through with variations twice before they sang it.

"That's not bad at all!" I whispered to Debra. "If they have any decent words to the music, they might win. Looks to me like the crowd is going for it as a real change of pace."

"Haven't you heard the words?"

"No. It's a deep secret—like the enigma of the sphinx. Jake would let his fingernails be pulled out before he would let anyone hear those words up to now. Here they come!"

Then in perfect harmony, Jake Buck and The Termites sang:

It was Sunday when my mother
Broke from prison in the rain.
When I went for her in my pickup truck
She was run over by a train!

Dear old Mother!
How I'll miss her!
Life will never be the same.
Now she's sleeping by the railroad track
Where her ghost can hear the train
Whistle
Blow!

The crowd didn't know what to make of it. At first they just sat there, and I said, "They're going to tar and feather the Termites!"

But I was wrong. They loved it. The place broke into a roar, and the Termites had to do that fool song three times to avoid a riot!

"Never underestimate the bad taste of American youth," I said to Debra as we hollered and shouted with the rest of them. "This will probably become the national fad and set music back in the Dark Ages again."

"It's better than 'Bay-beeeee! Bay-beeeee!'" she said, then nudged me. "Look, Barney, over there!"

I took a quick look and nearly fell over. The Leatherwoods were sitting right up near the front—Glen, Teena, Hawk, and Robin, with Rafe Darrow, of all people.

"Rafe Darrow!" I muttered gloomily. "She's at it, Debra! She's going to reform Rafe Darrow!"

Debra gave me her funny look, and I had to gulp and try to keep my eyes from glazing over.

"She's got the *easy* one," Debra said. "Rafe won't be hard to manage. Now, me, I've got the *real* problem."

I leaned forward. "Problem? You have a problem, Debra? What in the world is it?"

Then without warning, she kissed me right on the lips.

That girl was downright unsanitary! She smiled, then, looking right at me, said, *"You,* Barney Buck of Goober Holler!"

Now why would she have said a thing like that?

*If you've enjoyed **The Ozark Adventures,***
you'll want to read these additional series!

Forbidden Doors *(New! Fall 1994)*
As Rebecca and Scott discover the danger of the occult, they learn to put their trust in God.

#1 The Society 0-8423-5922-2

#2 The Deceived 0-8423-1352-4

The Last Chance Detectives ***(New! Fall 1994)***
Four young sleuths tackle local mysteries from their restored B-17 bomber—and develop faith in God's guidance. Also on video!

#1 Mystery Lights of Navajo Mesa 0-8423-2082-2

Choice Adventures
These books let you create the story by choosing your own plot! Join the Ringers in sixteen adventures, including these latest releases:

#13 Mountain Bike Mayhem 0-8423-5131-0

#14 The Mayan Mystery 0-8423-5132-9

#15 The Appalachian Ambush 0-8423-5133-7

#16 The Overnight Ordeal 0-8423-5134-5

McGee and Me!
Meet Nick Martin, a normal kid with an unusual friend: the lively, animated McGee! All titles also available on video.

#1 The Big Lie 0-8423-4169-2

#2 A Star in the Breaking 0-8423-4168-4

#3 The Not-So-Great Escape 0-8423-4167-6

#4 Skate Expectations 0-8423-4165-X

#5 Twister and Shout 0-8423-4166-8

#6 Back to the Drawing Board 0-8423-4111-0

#7 Do the Bright Thing 0-8423-4112-9

#8 Take Me Out of the Ball Game 0-8423-4113-7

#9 'Twas the Fight Before Christmas 0-8423-4114-5

#10 In the Nick of Time 0-8423-4122-6

#11 The Blunder Years 0-8423-4123-4

#12 Beauty in the Least 0-8423-4124-2